# Jac

*For Muriel, as ever*

# Jac

## Sam Adams

ylolfa

First impression: 2023
© Sam Adams & Y Lolfa Cyf., 2023

Cover image: *Mount Pleasant Road, Gilfach Goch*, Christopher Hall
Cover design: Tanwen Haf

ISBN: 978 1 80099 442 3

Published and printed in Wales
on paper from well-maintained forests by
Y Lolfa Cyf., Talybont, Ceredigion SY24 5HE
*e-mail* ylolfa@ylolfa.com
*website* www.ylolfa.com
*tel* 01970 832 304

ONCE, NOT ALL that long ago, the valley was empty, the few farms lying on or over the hills to the east and west. And it was small, insignificant even, a nook only, the slightest cleft in the hills, or as Mam, Jac's grandmother would have said, a *cil fach*. Its own small stream, rising among rushes and white puffs of cotton grass on the peaty sponge of the upland, had over millennia etched a narrow channel through a stray, red-tinted ironstone outcrop before tumbling silver down the steep slope that sealed its northern end. There, fed by copious rainfalls, it gathered strength to find a stony bed on the narrow, wooded bottom land. For centuries, the valley was, indeed, green, and the only sounds were those of the breeze through foliage and long grasses, birdsong, the barking of foxes on chill, moonlit winter nights, and the rippling of the glass-clear, trout-frequented stream.

If you had taken the trouble to look even then, and some did, here and there on grassy slopes among the bracken, perhaps where soil had crept downhill, were tell-tale black bruises and mineral glints. Coal was already mined in neighbouring valleys, why not in this? In a mere instant of the aeons since creation began, the valley's woods were felled for makeshift dwellings and props to secure the roofs of tunnels dug deep underground. Men and women came, families came with their household trappings, quarries scarring the bared mountainside gave their stone for more substantial homes, brief terraces of houses coalesced into straggling streets edging the broadened path that became a road cast like a noose around the lower slopes, and a railway line followed the river's route out into the world. The valley held a village in its cupped hand.

Not everyone who came prospecting found the thick black seams they sought. Trial shafts were sunk and levels driven into the hillside to produce nothing more than mounds of grey shale that remained as sprawled monuments to failure, while the slag-heaps of the three successful mines, many years in the piling, were barren, black mountain ranges rising steeply from the banks of the stream high enough to obscure the view of one side of the valley from the other. Wounded, bruised black, hacked and scarred, it lay under the ever-changing sky, and beneath its battered surface tunnels crawled further and deeper year by year. The men, who like burrowing creatures spent half their waking day, summer and winter, in these depths, bore the marks of their trade with the earth, a common pallor and blue scars, and were possessed of a strenuous loyalty to their butties, fellow workers who shared the exacting labour and its dangers.

This small world had a single purpose, a single reason for existence: the mining of coal. But the miners' outlay of labour (and what labour!) in return for pay was never a simple transaction and often a cause of bitter dispute. No decade was free of strife, strikes, violent confrontation, penury, hunger, suffering and loss. It was only in the late 1930s that what had seemed to be a permanent state of want, discord and unrest was ended by a common cause – the need to meet the threat of war. Then the valley's three pits worked three shifts a day, the air throbbed with the noise of production, the slag-heaps grew ever taller and wider, and the stream wound its way, black, at their foot.

*

When he thought back, Jac could remember very little before he found himself sweating and spotty in a tangle of sheets under an enormous weight of blankets. Perhaps it was the loneliness of the situation, hour after hour it seemed, with the bedroom door closed, that made him conscious of not only his sickly predicament but his separate self. He shouted but no-one came. He wept, still no-one. He wailed, to no purpose. He had been abandoned. He grew frustrated and angry, fought against the load of bedclothes and reached for the toy gun on the bedside chair, a cap pistol, bought to cheer him on his sickbed, with no caps. Half-sitting, he held it by the black handle and struck the wall on the other side of the bed with the silver barrel until he was coughing and quite breathless. Then, noticing the marks he had made in the pale, patterned wallpaper, a score or more half-moon indentations, laid the pistol carefully on the chair and shrank back under the blankets. What would his mother say?

His mother, his father, his already well-grown sister had always been there, like arms and legs extensions of himself, but now their absence made him keenly aware that they had a separate existence – as did he. There were other images, faint impressions of remote events, as though left over from sleep, that sometimes rose into his waking thoughts. He might seem to be passing shops along the familiar street, but it was not his mother who held his hand, nor his sister, Jo, who resented the imposition. Not his father, of course; his father was in work. It was Mam, his grandmother, who was no longer with them. There was a time when he was told to 'Hush' because Mam was in bed, even though it was the middle of the day. She was not very well. Then he was taken to the bedroom where she lay and Dada held him so that he could kiss her withered cheek. Her eyes were closed, but she knew who it was and the faintest smile came to her pale lips.

There was a picture of Mam on the landing, at the top of the stairs. It showed her with fair hair neatly pulled back, a high collar with an edge of lace and a small gold cross on a chain around her neck, a young woman. Now he had little recollection of her save voluminous dark skirts, a warm, tender, veined and bony hand and how she used to take him with her up the road. On their walks, she would pause to gossip with others, usually while he gazed at their shins and ankles. There was one shop doorway where they often stopped because, if it was fine, the very small, old woman, a friend of Mam and fellow Salvationist, would be standing there while her much larger son served behind the counter. Inside, the shop was somehow suffused with pale light and had its own special smell of savoury things and tea and sawdust. It was called 'Spearings'. Sometimes Mam bought pork pies there to be warmed in the oven for dinner with potatoes and gravy, but whether she was buying pies or not, she always stopped to talk with old Mrs Spearing, until Jac, bored, then restless, tugged at her hand and she allowed herself to be drawn away to some destination he had in mind. Perhaps it was to buy sweets, or a comic, the *Dandy*, or the *Beano*.

That thought stirred a precious fragment of recent memory, of sitting in the sun on the corrugated roof of the coalhouse, where it was low on the garden side, with Mama, his mother, looking at story strips and their speech bubbles, which she read to him, pointing at the words, with her soft voice and gentle laughter at the antics of Desperate Dan and Korky the Cat.

The front door of the house opened onto a sloping patch

of unkempt grass unevenly divided by a curving path of coal-dust-stained golden gravel, edged with terracotta tiles bearing a twisted rope design on the top edge. Stone walls, black with ubiquitous dust and mapped with stains of green mould, separated this patch of garden from its neighbours on either side, and the pink blossoms of a rambler rose festooning the wall near the door once each summer surprised callers with the strength and sweetness of their perfume. A circular plot of modest size in the larger portion of grass had long before been seeded with perennials that struggled unhappily against encroaching daisies, producing ever fewer and smaller flowers as year followed year.

A row of grey semis stood over the road. Beyond them was the railway line, and then, the source of constant clanking noise, a black inclined embankment, which hid from view all but the upper reaches of the mountain on 'the other side'. Journeys of loaded drams were hauled slowly up the incline to the colliery screens for sorting slag and dirt from the coal they carried, and clattered empty down. The door at the back of the house opened to a view of the mountain: you needed only to walk up the garden path, unlatch the creaking gate, and in another dozen short steps, there you were, climbing on tussocky grass towards a high, green horizon and encircling sky.

Inside, the house had four bedrooms. The door of one, at the back of the house over the kitchen, was usually closed. That had been Mam's bedroom. There was a landing window, which on bright days in late spring and summer caught the sun as it rose above the mountain so that a distinct beam of light full of dancing dust motes shone down the stairs, gleaming along the dark, polished dado rail and glossy, white-painted anaglypta with its raised pattern below. Above the rail was a wallpaper of mauves and dusky pinks and dark green, foliage perhaps, and fruit, and on it hung a picture of an autumn-tinted lakeside scene with Highland cattle.

Jac's bedroom was the smallest. It had two windows. One, a large sash window, overlooked the house next door, its paved backyard, a washing line and, if he turned his head to look to the right, a walled garden and a part of the steep, green mountain slope beyond with the reddish-brown gash of an old quarry. The other, of eight small panes, was set too high for him to see out, unless he brought the chair to clamber on, but he knew it had a view of a pair of the grey, roughcast-rendered houses in the row on the other side of the road. His bed, tight against the wall opposite the smaller window, shared the room with a rattan-seated bedside chair and a bow-fronted mahogany chest, which had three wide, deep drawers well-filled with spare blankets and sheets, and two smaller drawers at the top that were intriguingly out of his reach.

Almost every man in the village physically able to work in a coal mine did. That was the reason men had brought their families there in the first place and, in due turn, sons followed their fathers' lead, clumping alongside them in unfamiliar, new working-boots. The teacher would ask the class of older boys what they wanted to do when they left school and nearly every one would say 'Go with my father down the pit'. Few failed to keep that promise. Jac's turn would come when he reached fourteen, because the law said you couldn't leave school until you reached that age.

For Jac's father it had been when he was twelve. And then he went not as a collier at the coal face; he was lucky because he was interested in mechanical things and quick to learn about the new electrical machines that were coming in. He was employed in the Squint, where the coal that filled the drams crawling up the incline not far over the road was mined by men Jac heard tramping the early morning darkness with a rhythmic crunch of steel-shod soles on road and pavement, as though some great beast were chewing away at life, after the mournful hooter calling them to work stirred his measles-restless sleep. His father's working-clothes and cap had their places on hooks in the shallow alcove by the back door, where the mustiness of coal lurked, a faint residue of the ancient rotted vegetation that had metamorphosed into polished black lumps and glistening dust. If more fully awake, prompted perhaps by a need to use the chamber pot under the bed, he would hear his father rattling the big kitchen grate with the poker to dislodge the remains of yesterday's fire, and then scraping together and shovelling cinders and fine grey dust into a bucket to be collected by the ashman on his weekly round. In a little while, before putting his boots on and leaving for work, as soundlessly as he could, Dada would come upstairs with a cup of tea and place it on the bedside chair in the room where Mama lay.

His mother's bedroom had a sash-window overlooking the garden at the back of the house that was so large it would tremble and seem to bend when rowdy autumn winds bullied the valley. The room had a big bed, a wardrobe, a mirrored dressing table, and a marble-topped washstand on which stood a bowl and, in it, a large jug patterned with flowers that could be filled with water for pouring into the bowl to wash the sleep out of your eyes in the morning, though they were rarely used, for there was a bathroom along the landing. Beyond the bathroom was the bedroom of Jac's much older sister, Josephine, known to everyone in the family and outside as 'Jo'.

'Jacob' was the name inscribed on Jac's birth certificate, the name he had been given at his christening, which had followed painfully close upon his grandfather's sudden death. The old man had a terrible wheezing chest, the consequence of many years' work underground in stone dust and coal dust, but was always cheerful and never saw a doctor, so that when he died quietly in the middle of an afternoon nap, it was a profound shock to the family and all who knew him. A crowd of silent men trooped after his hearse. Mama, barely recovered from an unexpected pregnancy and arduous birth, so soon followed by the death and burial of a man she, too, had grown to love and respect for his calm good humour, had no clear idea what name to give the infant.

Mam, newly widowed, looking towards the heavens and wiping a tear, said, 'Well, haven't we been given a name? Surely he's Jacob (she pronounced it the Welsh way), like his *Tad-cu*.'

It was Jo who early on decided to call her baby brother 'Jac', on the principle that if a two-letter abbreviation was good enough for her, three would certainly do for him. She shrugged and hid her pride when Mama, who thought 'Jacob' (the English way) old-fashioned, and was scathing about 'Jake', after a little thought said, 'Jack will do nicely.'

'Yes, of course,' his grandmother added, unexpectedly, when news of this came to her, 'J-A-C, Jac – short for Jacob.' And that settled matters. Jac's mother, Edith, was 'Ede', for so his father called to her if she wasn't in the kitchen when he came home from work, and he was 'Tom', for so she stirred him when in the evening, having nodded off before the fire, he began to snore. Tom and Ede, Jo and Jac – nothing grand about the names, plain and serviceable monosyllables all.

*

Dinah was the fifth member of the household. There was always a dog, in the beginning to keep Ede company and give reassurance when Tom was called out in the night, as happened quite often. They would be startled awake in the dark depths by loud hammering on the door. Tom would struggle into his pit clothes, knowing what awaited him outside: a breathless collier anxious to convey the bad news, that some vital machine, over-burdened, or simply old and worn, had broken down. He was needed immediately. With hardly time to lace his boots properly, he would be running down the road to the Squint to plunge into the deeper darkness of the pit. There, his wits needed to be sharp for all dangers, while his knowledge and skill were put to the test again. It might be many hours before he returned to the surface and could plod wearily home.

How much comfort a dog could have brought in his absence is hard to tell. Whether Dinah brought any was doubtful – except that, once she was fully grown, any marauder in the vicinity would have thought twice about risking an attempt at the unbolted door, or even a polite knock. She grew from a nervous black pup with a docked tail to a broad-backed heavyweight with bandy front legs, enormous dangling ears and a ferocious presumption of possession. The house and everything in it was hers. This naturally included any item delivered through the letterbox, daily newspaper or morning post. As with all dogs, her hearing was acute. A finger touch on the latch of the front gate was enough to rouse her from slumber, or lift her head from her breakfast bowl, and bring her at a gallop from the kitchen to the hall where, braking, she would skid over the polished red tiles, thud against the door jaws ajar and catch whatever dropped through the letterbox. The scratching of claws on tile and the thumping collision of dog and door were familiar to Jac, who slept in the small room above the hall. By itself, this would have been an acceptable part of morning routine, but once she had seized the delivery Dinah was very reluctant to relinquish it. The family suffered her foibles and rages on the grounds that she kept the nefarious and undesirable at bay, even if she constantly failed to distinguish between any such and entirely welcome relatives and friends. Therein lay a problem never satisfactorily solved until, grown old, the dog decided to devote her remaining energies to looking after the ducks.

*

Jo had been a sickly infant, so often laid low with fevers that her tearful parents more than once despaired of her survival. But having at last gained a firm grip on life, she grew vigorous, if not greatly in stature, determined and quite fearless. This resoluteness did not extend to work in school, but there was something about her bold self-possession that persuaded teachers she did well enough as it was and further intervention, punitive or pedagogic, was not required. Ten when Jac was born, and not yet grown out of tomboyhood, she was devoted to horse-riding. She seemed to have inherited the skills of her great-uncles, both of whom, before they passed on, had been hauliers working underground. Horses large and small, reassured by her firm, no-nonsense regard for them, were content to be guided by her and did as she commanded. She became acquainted with others of about her age who owned or borrowed ponies, among them an admiring circle of rough boys from the top of the valley. Her dainty proportions were deceptive. She was strong and quick, and they were wary of her, for she was known to have a flaring temper and a mean way with a switch.

It was not that Jo disliked her brother. There was no spiteful jealousy in her: she didn't feel he had replaced her in her parents' affections. On the whole, she was indifferent to him. What she resented was the expectation that she should spend time amusing him or taking him for walks. Pushing the pram in which he lay wrapped-up sleeping was humiliation enough; if he was awake and (God forbid!) crying, it was worse than the serpent's sting. Sometimes, she would call on a school friend similarly burdened, and they would walk and push together, filling the pavement and ignoring passers-by, especially cooing, inquisitive older women who wanted to peep under the hood to see how the little one was getting on.

With company the chore became bearable. Jo even enjoyed occasions when the babies were lulled to sleep by the motion of the prams and they strolled away from the few shops and prying people. From time to time, especially when the weather was fine, they would walk to the big cemetery serving the village and the area around, which had many hundreds of graves. If the wind was in the right direction, you might occasionally hear in the distance the stertorous gasps of a steam-engine hauling away another long line of trucks loaded with coal, but the cemetery was usually deserted and silent apart from buzzing insects and birdsong in the surrounding trees and hedges. Within tall, ornamental gates it had a broad central avenue climbing a gentle slope off which, on either side, narrower paths ran and intersected, so that, viewed from above, it might have looked rather like the pattern of an eccentric board game where players picked a route from the several variants available to arrive first at an agreed point. At least, that was what Jo proposed on their first pram-pushing visit, and it became a regular feature – a kind of chariot race that she found hugely enjoyable. The two girls would set off along different paths, each walking smartly with one eye on the progress of her competitor. Usually, within twenty yards, Jo had begun to trot and, seeing her friend take up the challenge, in twenty more both would be running full-pelt, skimming marble curbs at tight corners, the prams swaying and jolting, until they skidded to a halt breathless and helpless with laughter at the finishing post, while fading flowers in grave pots shook their heads in dismay and the thoroughly shaken babies howled.

'Oh dear, oh dear, what's the matter then?' the girls would say, with feigned sympathy and concern, patting and rocking and pacifying until the cries calmed to a whimper and then silence once more. It was little wonder that Jac came to regard Jo with a mixture of love, admiration for her energetic daring, and wary watchfulness. For her part, Jo couldn't wait for him to grow enough to enjoy a rough and tumble, even to go riding with her. Perhaps if they had been nearer in age, they would have come naturally to dispute over toys, or books, or nothing, and to pinches and pushes and slaps and wrestling, as children do. But Jac knew he was outmatched in every respect, and if ever there was a contest – over the last slice of cake at teatime, perhaps – he would protest tearfully and, for the sake of peace, more often than not had his way.

*

Jac had been taken for walks on the mountain almost as soon as he was able to totter a few steps without falling over. Jo was wiry and strong and when she ran out of excuses to avoid looking after him – and, anyway, was glad to get out of the house for a while – she would take him by the hand and they would leave by the creaking, grinding back-garden gate. Outside they crossed a broad, black path of well-trodden ash from a steam-driven pit engine-house a mere fifty yards off on the right, of which only low walls and a huge iron winding-wheel remained. Long ago, the pit had failed, though not before re-shaping the green hillside around with tips of grey shale. Jo and Jac turned left, off the packed ash onto a narrower grassy path that led diagonally up the mountain, past an abandoned quarry to a wooden bench seat, where Jac, already weary and complaining at the pace his sister set, could play with a toy car and rest while she looked out over the valley. From this vantage point, above the barrier of the nearby tips and the incline to the screens, she could see the nucleus and fulcrum of the village, black and full of the clattering and clanging life of its three pits, and hear its regular heartbeat in the thud-thud-thud of steam-driven air compressors.

Grown-ups with a little time to spare and no rain in prospect might be tempted to go for a stroll on the mountain, but rarely beyond that few yards of level ground where the bench was perched. Above, where the path wound higher, was another country, largely inhabited by sheep – and, on dry weekends, long summer evenings and holidays, by children. There, out of sight, under a cloud-hung sky, with no fences and no-one to warn or admonish them, they did as they pleased and their imagination prompted. In time, as Jac's legs grew somewhat longer and stronger, he plodded after Jo up another diagonal path to a higher point where they would sit on the coarse, shaggy grass and look down on the serpentine extension of terraces under their scaly slated roofs winding along the valley's flanks, the muted collieries in the midst, gushes of white smoke rising, and glimpses of river and railway line between the towering tips, all miniature, a grubby toy village.

'Where's our house?' Jac would ask and Jo, with unusual patience, would point and say, 'Do you see there, the path we came up, and the old bench? There, look, there – and the path going down then, past the quarry?' Jac would nod. 'And at the end of that, just where it meets the black path – across there – that's our house!'

'Oh, yes. I can see it!' And the sense of security thrilled him with inward joy.

In time, even longer walks took them higher still, over the crest of the hill, so that the entire valley disappeared. But on that upland they could view, a long way off, distant places, smoky smudges that were other villages and their pits, and especially on sunny days, if they looked to the south, bright flashes of reflected light.

'Do you know what that is shining, right over by there?' said Jo, pointing to the horizon.

Jac shook his head.

'That's the sea!'

On just such a day, a little breathless from their climb, Jo and Jac lay on the grass, out of the breeze. They were looking up at an intensely blue sky crossed by a stuttering trail of white clouds, just like puffs from a heavenly steam engine, when Jac became aware of a sound, a wonderful, sustained trilling, falling to them from the sky, birdsong he knew, but of a kind he had never heard before.

'What's that Jo?'

'It's a bird. If you look carefully, right up above us, you might see it.'

And they looked and Jac saw, high, suspended in the cloud-hung blue of the sky, a tiny, fluttering dark shape.

'Is that it?'

'Yes. Yes, that's the one. That little dot up there. It's a lark,' she said, ' – a skylark. Its nest is somewhere near, in the grass. I've looked before, but never found one. It's got a lovely song.'

'Oh, yes,' said Jac, as the sweet, tremulous, twittering notes trickled down through the air like some revivifying potion.

Having spent many hours riding on her own or with friends along remoter high paths, Jo knew lots of things about the mountain, but usually didn't have the patience to share her knowledge with her brother.

She sat up. 'See that wall over there,' she said, pointing to a line of stones climbing a gentle slope patchily covered with dark-green half-grown bracken like clumps of furled umbrellas. 'That was built by the Romans.'

There were, indeed, the remains of a wall, broken almost to the ground in parts, with big tumbled stones spotted and patched with gold and silver lichen half hidden in the grass nearby. Jac's eyes opened wide. He had never heard of Romans, but there was that special note of emphasis in Jo's voice that told him this was precious information.

'The Romans conquered England, and everywhere they

went they built roads, and walls – like that one. Then they came to conquer us. So our side got their men together and they had a big fight with the Romans on the mountain, and our side won. Over there, up the top of the valley – see? – just below where that sort of tump is on the mountain.'

Jac nodded.

'Well, just by there's a boggy patch where Bonny sinks down to her fetlocks.'

Again Jac nodded, eyes still wide, mouth too, as he waited for the story to continue.

'And water trickles away from it in a little stream, and – do you know what? – that water is red. And they say that's where the Romans were all killed and their blood ran down the mountain. And – do you know what?'

Jac shook his head. Whatever his sister was about to say, he was sure he didn't know.

'That's why this place is called Gilfach Goch, "Little red valley", in Welsh, because of all the blood from the Romans.'

'So that was the end of them,' said Jac, releasing his breath with a big sigh, satisfied with this outcome.

'Yes – but their walls are still here – a bit broken, because it's been ages and ages.'

Jac was waiting for the story to continue, but Jo got up. 'Come on,' she said, catching his hand and pulling him to his feet, 'let's go and see what's for tea.'

She walked back to the hill crest and, pausing for a moment at the top of the steep slope overlooking the valley, she stretched her arms wide and leaned against the freshening breeze. Then, with hair streaming behind like some minor deity of the place, she let herself fall into running and bounding from tussock to tussock, down, down to the very foot. It was over in a flash and there she was, a diminutive figure waving to Jac from the back-garden gate. He longed to follow her light-footed descent, but decided the diagonals of the well-trodden path were safer. As he trotted along them he thought of his sister's tale about the Romans. He believed it, and she may have believed it herself.

★

The measles had struck soon after Jac started school, an unwanted initiation gift. His big sister had been asked to take him on his first day, because Mama's leg was painful and, since Jo, who was going to the 'Big School' across the road from the Infants', was on her way at about the same time and in the same direction, it wouldn't be a hardship. She flounced and fretted, which was only to be expected, but was persuaded she would need to do it only once, to make sure Jac knew the way and arrived in time. His mother bent to hoist his coat so that it fitted him properly and straighten the collar, for it was misty and damp outside, and kissed his cheek.

'Now, be a good boy,' she said. 'Listen to the teacher. We'll have your dinner ready when you come home and you can tell me all that you've done in the morning. Your boots look lovely – just like Dada's.' They had been bought with money saved on the Co-op Club book, and Jac's father had got out his last and hammered a pattern of studs in the soles. She had polished them until they glowed. 'There – give your hand to Jo. Now off you go.'

Jo took the proffered hand with only a hint of demur and set off, hurrying so that Jac trotted to keep up, while Mama, leaning against the squat brick pillar where the front gate was squeakily hinged, waved at the receding backs of her children and wiped her eyes.

The walk to school took them past the shop in which Jac sometimes spent pennies on sweets, around the corner, down a slight slope where, on the right, the other side of the road, stood a grand cinema, and over the bridge above the railway tracks. Just there, below them, long lines of trucks always stood waiting to be filled with coal or, loaded, for a steam-engine to be hooked on at the front and hauled away. If you were lucky and an engine puffed under the bridge as you were passing over, great white gusts jetted up around your knees through gaps between the narrow pavement and the corrugated sheets lining its edge. After the bridge, an unnaturally straight road, one the Romans would have been proud of, crossed the valley and then, with terraced houses left and right, climbed the slope the other side, almost to the school gate.

Older children in the yard were chasing one another with shouts and screams and a handful of new pupils, with their gossiping mothers, were gathered around a door above which 'Infants' was etched in a grimy slab of pale stone. Jo didn't join in the adult talk. She thrust the folded note with his name and address into her brother's hot hand and saying, 'Give it to the teacher,' left abruptly.

Jac stood with head bowed on the fringe of the group shuffling his studs on the tarmac. In a while a teacher opened the door, looked out over the yard, rang a handbell vigorously and, smiling, 'Come on in then,' she said, 'let's get you settled.'

The mothers briefly examined their children. One or two wiped traces of breakfast at the corners of mouths with a little spit on a handkerchief, which seemed a kind of blessing, and after brief hugs and a few words thrust them forward. Jac held out his crumpled note and the teacher said, 'For me? Oh, I see. Thank you. Go on in.'

A little later, in a classroom with long, low tables around which the children were sitting in diminutive wooden tub chairs, a few with heads on arms sobbing quietly, Miss Jones was taking the register. Nearing the end of her list, 'Jacob Williams?' she said, and paused, looking around the seated infants, then rather louder, 'Jacob Williams?'

'He's Jac, Miss.' The voice came from a little girl, Jac's cousin, from the top of the valley, whom he barely knew, already veteran of a whole term in school.

'Oh, Jac is it? H'm. Jac Williams?'

'Yes, Miss.'

And so the name was fixed, among family, in school, with friends and new acquaintance, around the valley, for any occasion and all time.

*

Reasonably enough, the larger room at the front of the house was called 'the front room'. It was Jac's favourite, especially on an evening when the fire was lit. It had a comfortable three-piece suite covered in moquette densely patterned with climbing tendrils pale and darker green. Over the fireplace was a large mirror, which reflected the mirrored sideboard against the opposite wall. Quite soon after he began to notice such things, Jac found that if he stood on the settee, holding on to the back to stop himself bouncing off, and looked in either of the mirrors he would see himself, his face and the back of his head alternately, and much of the room, repeated endlessly because the mirrors did not know how to stop reflecting one another. It was a wonder – and a puzzle – with his image going on forever.

A window in the same room looked out over the front railings to the pairs of houses over the road and, between them, a brief section of the black incline climbing to the colliery screens. Against the wall opposite, glowing in the window's light, stood the handsome, polished case of an upright piano. When all the needful work of the day, washing and cleaning and preparing meals, was done, Mama would slip away to the front room and pick something out from the bundle of sheet music stored in the piano stool and play for a while. If it was raining, or cold and winter-dark, and Jac was indoors, he would soon be drawn to watch and listen. He marvelled how his mother's eyes were always on the pages of lines and dancing dots while her fingers deftly found their own way to the black and white keys. She had learned to play as a child, because (she told him) her father, whom Jac had never knowingly seen, loved music. 'He said we all had to learn to play an instrument – all my sisters and brothers, your aunties and uncles. But most of them didn't keep it up when they started work.'

'He played the violin,' she would say. 'I remember when they first opened the hall where you go to the pictures now, and they had an orchestra for the opening. A lot of very good players – some of them had come from other places round about. And he was the conductor. And there was such clapping.' Then, wistfully, 'He was a very good violinist, and I used to accompany him.'

Jac wasn't sure what it all meant, but he knew by her voice that his mother was moved by the memory.

The big family to which she belonged had dispersed over the

24

years, moved on and moved away, with the single exception of a younger sister, whom Jac knew as Aunty Lil. She and Uncle Percy lived in what had been the family home (though how that whole crowd of aunts and uncles, even when they were quite small, had been packed into the terraced house was beyond conjecture). When the couple first married they had come there as company for Lilian's recently widowed mother, and as time went on they stayed to care for her. Jac had a faint memory of a benign, silver-haired, older woman sitting in a corner of a settee regarding him closely and saying, 'I don't think he looks much like you, Edith.'

Before her leg became too painful to tackle the hill, Mama would take Jac up the road to see her sister. Aunty Lil was always there and sometimes Uncle Percy too, if he was not in work. They had no children. Bald, smiling and gentle, Percy, who, like so many others, spent eight-hour days underground in a coal mine when hardly more than a child, had a chest that wheezed like a broken concertina. That might have brought an early end to his days in the colliery, but his calm confidence with horses recommended him to a place among the blacksmiths, for shoeing pit ponies was an important part of the job. He was not, and never would be, a brawny-armed 'mighty man' like the smith in the old poem Jac later heard at school, but lean and wiry: without sinew and strength he would not have survived an hour slogging on his knees at the coal face. The new job couldn't cure his dreadful cough, but in the blacksmiths' shop he quickly learned the essential skills of sizing, forging, shaping and fitting horseshoes, and sharpening tools and repairing metal parts, so there he stayed.

Aunty Lil, small and thin and 'always on the go', had greying dark hair, big brown eyes and a wide, lovely smile. Whenever

Jac visited (later he would come on his own on errands or because he just felt like), she would make a fuss of him. He would have to sit at the table and have a glass of milk and a biscuit, or sometimes tinned sardines on toast, and tell her what he had been up to and what he was doing in school, and she would watch him closely as he ate and smile when his eyes met hers.

*

The shed where Jac's father kept his motorbike had been built as a stable for the pit ponies that hauled the laden drams of the now abandoned colliery close behind the house, the only building still standing. There would have been room enough for four horses in separate stalls, but the mangers and wooden partitions had long before been broken up and used as firewood. All that remained was a high, covered space and the floor of salt-glazed brown paviours with an incised diamond pattern for sweeping clean with stiff brushes. When its big, double doors were open, you could look out over a small but convenient patch of firm ash to the ruins of the colliery's engine house enclosing a great iron winding-wheel, too large to be conveniently hauled away when all the rest of the machinery had been scrapped. The shed's corrugated sheeting had been preserved over the years by thick, black coats of bitumen paint, though rust had enlarged a small gap close to the crest of the roof on the side exposed to the worst of the wind and weather, and numerous nail holes, through which, on fine days, the sun streamed in slim searchlight beams.

The bike was Dada's pride and joy, Jac's mother told him. He looked after it with care, even tenderness. 'Just the way

I look after you,' she added, cwtching him in her arms. The number of families in the village that had a car you could count on the fingers of a hand – and have a few to spare. All around the valley, wives and mothers dreamed of family trips to the seaside, especially in a car, sheltered from wind and rain, with room for everyone. But it was out of the question. Fortunately, someone could always be relied on to organise a charabanc trip at least once a year and, if those who could afford to add their names to the list were lucky, on a really nice day. Everyone agreed that a bike was easier to maintain and cheaper to run than a car, but even this lesser ambition was beyond the means of most.

With a hint of pride, Dada referred to his bike as 'the old 'Arley'. It wore an unpretentious coat of khaki paint, was as sturdy as a pit pony – and a good deal noisier. With the breeze steady and from the right direction you would hear its bubbling roar almost as soon as it entered the valley on its way back to the black shed. What had persuaded him to buy that bike was the large boat-shaped sidecar, with a small door at the side for ease of entry and a comfortable seat and weatherproof cover for the passenger, so that he and Ede could go for a run together, as they often did before Jo was born. More remarkably, when Jo and, much later Jac, too, would come, because he couldn't very well be left behind, the sidecar had a dicky that you could unclip and pull out to accommodate a child, or even two, if they were not over-large. Jo and Jac, properly wrapped up for the open air and the wind of speed, shared the little bench seat of the dicky, on fine holiday outings, before the war.

Every working day, Jac's father was busy with clever hands and fingers keeping the colliery's many machines in working order, often in awkward corners underground, by weak lamplight, and sometimes, when it was the pumps that had failed, up to his waist in water. But at weekends he could still find pleasure in stripping down the bike, replacing or repairing as necessary, topping up the oil, greasing moving parts and putting all neatly together again. The big hollow of the shed echoed with the tapping and clinking of his work, and the air bore the odours of old bike oil laced with the occasional sweet pungency of petrol.

While he was contentedly absorbed, Jac would potter about the shed, for many metal objects of varying shapes and sizes, bits of earlier bikes long since sold on, or broken-up for spares, lay in out-of-the-way corners. They could be strange objects in a desert, glistening steel ramparts overthrown with a metallic clatter, smoothly hollowed caves through which a hero could creep, monstrous engines in an alien landscape, like that which Flash Gordon descended upon from his spaceship in the Saturday morning matinée serial that Jac sometimes saw when Jo could be persuaded to take him. There was besides an array of spanners and screwdrivers, pliers and pincers, hammers and hacksaws, hand drills and wrenches; a multitude of nails and screws and small, nameless metal objects in a big wooden box, a work bench with a vice for holding things steady while they were screwed together or unscrewed, cut with a saw or ground with a file, and a sandstone wheel on a stand for sharpening tools. 'Come and see this,' Dada would say from time to time. Then he might show how the bike's brakes worked or, pointing, recite the names of parts of the engine, but it all seemed complicated and difficult to remember. So Jac would stand and watch silently while his father's strong, broad hands ('like shovels' Mama said), and thick fingers, stained with oil and dirt, deftly did their work, and bent the intricacies of the machine to his will.

One sunny, quiet spring Sunday morning, the colliery almost silent, for only teams of repair men were working, Jac's father said he would go up to the shed while dinner was cooking and bring the bike round to the front, in case they felt like a short trip, a breath of air, before teatime. Jac went with him. The shed door, opened wide, revealed the bike tilted to one side, back wheel off the ground, resting on its kickstand. It was the work of a moment to set the bike four-square on the floor and then wheel it out of the shed. In the brief silence that followed, Jac suddenly became aware of birds twittering somewhere above his head. He looked up and was surprised to see, where a chance ray of sunlight had hit upon it, a clay cup plastered to the broad wooden beam that ran the length of the shed. Even before he noticed a bird slipping at speed through the narrow gap under the crest and flying to it, and although he had never seen one before, he knew at once it was a nest.

'Dada,' he called, 'come and see. It's a nest – a nest, a birds' nest!'

His father was about to start the bike, busy with his hands here and there, then pressing down on the starting pedal a few times before, with a little jump, kicking down on it hard. As the engine roared into life a gout of flame appeared at the exhaust followed by billowing smoke, then he was busy with his hands once more and the engine settled to its usual throaty rumble.

'What's that you said?'

'It's a nest, a birds' nest – up there, on the rafter.'

The twittering could not be heard above the noise of the bike, but quick fluttering flashes of dark blue and white plumage were again caught in sunlight beams as the parent birds hastened to and from the nest.

'See?' he said, pointing. 'What birds are those?'

His father, ambling in, thought a moment. 'Martins,' he said. 'At least, I think they are. Yes, I'm sure. They're house martins – catching flying insects outside and bringing them to the young ones. They're having dinner early.'

As they watched, once again a bird flew through the narrow gap as though it were wide as a road to perch on the edge of the nest. It was met by a chorus of twittering audible even above the rolling growl of the engine outside.

'Can I go up and see inside the nest?'

Two ladders lay against the bottom of the back wall of the shed, one an extension ladder for reaching right up the side of the house, the other a light roof-ladder. Jac had seen his father climb up the tall extension ladder to the very top, carrying the roof ladder in one hand, and somehow hooking it to the crest of the roof, before clambering down again to fetch slates. Once on the roof, he was out of sight, though you could hear his hammer striking the broad-headed clout nails he used to fix fresh slates in place.

'What's Dada doing?' he had asked.

'Mending the roof, of course!' Which was as much by way of explanation as he had the right to expect from his sister, who was always busy doing something else.

Now he said again to his father, 'Can I go up the small ladder and look?'

'I don't think it will reach that far. You can watch them from here.'

'But there are baby birds in the nest. I can hear them, only I can't see them.'

His father looked perplexed. 'I don't think your mother would want you climbing up ladders,' he said. 'Come on, the bike's ready. Let's go and have dinner.'

'Please Dada, I can climb a ladder,' Jac said.

It was true, up to a point. Goaded by Jo, he had some time ago climbed the steep, ladder-like steps to the top of the slide in the park, and more recently, on one of the evenings his father, who liked dozing by the fireside, rather reluctantly spent redecorating the front room, he had taken advantage of an opportunity to climb a tall step ladder, with Mama at its foot, arms extended, ready to catch him if he missed his footing.

'All right then. But you be very careful. I'll have to see if the ladder will reach first.'

Jac saw, with a small thrill of anticipated pleasure, that it did. But the hooks at its top refused to loop over the beam.

'Look ...' his father began, then, 'Oh, never mind. Come on, I'll hold it steady.'

Jac found the rungs more widely spaced than his limited experience had prepared him for. Although eager to climb, he made slow, ungainly progress, using his arms to pull himself upwards from step to step. As he neared the top he looked down, meaning to signal his success to his father. It was then he saw how far he was from the floor, higher than the park slide. He felt his knees shake.

'Can you see the young ones?'

'Nearly,' he said, weakly, placing his foot on another rung.

As he hauled himself up to the level of the nest, he was struck with wonder. There were indeed little birds, fully fledged or near it. He had no time to count how many – four? five? – for the instant before he saw them, they had seen his head rise at the lip of the nest and now burst out together, fluttering madly in different directions.

Shocked by the feathered fountain, Jac started back, lost his grip on one side rail as his foot slid from the supporting rung and found himself hanging in space as one leg of the ladder lifted from the floor. He was too shocked to utter a sound, but held on for the second it took for a firm hand and a strong arm to press the foot of the ladder back securely to the paviours.

In the strange silence that filled the empty spaces of the shed, Jac's father breathed deeply.

'Are you all right?' he said.

There was no reply, but he could see Jac had regained his hold and his footing.

'Can you come down?'

Again there was no reply, but Jac began to turn around to descend as he was used to doing on the steps of the slide in the park, when he just didn't feel like sliding.

'No! Not like that! Hold the sides and come down backwards.'

It was then, the momentary nightmare of hanging in space over, Jac began to weep, but very slowly, feeling for the rung below with one foot then the other, he began the descent. He was still several feet from the floor when his father, greatly relieved, caught him under the arms, lifted him away from the ladder and set him on the ground.

'Well, that was an adventure!' his father said, with another great sigh of relief. 'Perhaps we'd better go home and tell Mama about it.' And, as the boy raised his tear-stained face,

'Come on. We'll switch the engine off and leave the bike where it is till after dinner.'

Jac was glad to hold his father's hand as they walked slowly back down the rutted black path, past the grey shale tips to the familiar groaning back gate.

*

It was Saturday. The day had begun with showers of scattershot, wind-driven rain rattling against the kitchen windows, but by mid-morning some high breeze was sending curled scraps of white cloud tumbling across the sky's exhibition shades of blue, from pale at the mountain rim to azure overhead. The mountain itself in its shaggy coat of still uncertain green, holed and slag-scabbed, had not recovered from its winter pallor. Dirt-grey ewes, bulky with lamb, browsed without enthusiasm on tufts of grass.

Jac was twtied-down in the garden, digging aimlessly in a patch of still damp, black earth and starting back on his heels from time to time as his trowel uncovered the moist, pink squirm of a worm, or a millipede that curled itself in a ring, or a small, struggling black beetle. If he cared to look up, beyond the back wall topped with strung wire intended to keep out marauding sheep, he could see the old quarry from which stone to build the wall had come, where the soil was quite red. It had never occurred to him to wonder about this: was it the ubiquitous, ever-present coal dust that caused the blackness of the garden, or was it some kind of magic transformation that spilled from forking-in loads of horse manure? Jo's horse could be relied upon to produce ample supplies of the chaff-speckled, straw-strewn, soft brown rolls of sweet-smelling dung that Dada carried by the sackful down from the stable.

On the other side of the roughly-cobbled path, grey-bearded Dic John, a burly retired collier, bent with age and toil, who earned a shilling or two on odd days in spring and summer helping out in the garden, was preparing the ground for seeding with potatoes and runner beans. To Jac, who had two cousins near his own age both called John, the old man's name was confusing: it must really be John Dic, he thought. That his mother referred to him as 'Mister John' was a polite confirmation of the notion. There, anyway, in waistcoat and collarless flannel shirt, the sleeves rolled up, with boots from his days working underground, and yorks below his trouser knees from habit, old Dic was forking and turning over the soil. Progress was slow, for every yard or so of digging he was seized with a paroxysm of coughing.

When he had caught his breath after the latest fit, 'Jac, dere 'ma,' the old man called.

Jac was familiar with the Welsh words because he remembered how Mam would call to him as he ran about, 'Come here lovely boy', and catch him in her arms saying, 'Dere 'ma, cariad' softly in his ear as she held him close. Dic was leaning on his garden fork, his breath coming in peculiar wheezes and rattling gasps (for, like Uncle Percy, working life had given him more than pit boots and yorks).

'You've got a really nasty cold,' said Jac, his voice full of solicitude, like his mother's when he complained of not feeling well.

'Cold? Duw, no, bach. It's the old dust.'

Jac surveyed the forked, broken soil at their feet and nodded sympathetic understanding. He wasn't sure how it was making the old man cough, but perhaps it was just because he was old. Dada had a cough, too. He sometimes heard his father in the mornings, coughing and coughing while he was shovelling ashes from the grate and lighting the fire.

Dic had lifted the peak of his flat cap from his thinning grey curls and was scratching his head as he peered at a corner of the green-tinged wall, where a spider's web hung. It was not elegantly symmetrical, as many are, but a jumble of infinitely fine threads and, as Jac at once saw, it was vibrating.

'Look,' the old man said, pointing to a leaf fragment the night's squalls had blown into the web and now, at each fresh breath of breeze, was tugging this way and that like a live thing desperate to escape.

'See – this is spoiling all her plans.' He pointed to a small spider with a blob-like body and long front legs that seemed to be inspecting the leaf, which was dozens of times bigger than her. 'With that dangling and shivering there, she can never know if a fly comes into the web. What do you think she's up to?'

Jac shook his head.

'Let's wait a minute and find out.'

The creature was so small Jac couldn't discern what it was doing as it moved purposefully around, but gradually, as he watched, he saw that the leaf was being freed until eventually it hung by a single thread, and then, almost as though the spider had given it a final push, broke loose and floated away.

'How did it do that?' Jac was fascinated but baffled as the spider clambered back to her watchful corner crevice.

'Well,' said Dic, 'my old eyes can't see them, but yours might if you looked carefully enough, or if we had a magnifying glass perhaps we both could: she's got sharp jaws for such a little thing and she has chewed through the threads of her web that were holding the leaf, all the way round, until with a final big bite it was cut loose. Now isn't that clever?' He had a gruff old man's voice and was still breathing hard after his exertions. 'She had a problem with that leaf stuck there and she thought, "What can I do? Ah, I know", and, there you are, just as we were watching, she did it.'

'I would have thought of that,' said Jac.

'But you're a big boy, and you go to school, while she is a tiny creature; her whole body's no bigger than your fingernail. Let me see your teeth.' Jac curled his lips in a gappy grin. 'Yes – let's think … H'm. When you've got all your new teeth, I wonder – could you cut a web as neatly as she did? And remember, if it was your web, every string of it would be thick – thick as rope.'

Jac practised biting an imaginary rope. 'I don't think so,' he conceded. 'Yes, she is clever – and strong.'

'Bachgen da,' said Dic, smiling. 'There's a good boy. Now back to work with us.'

*

On another gardening day, Dic called him to see an ants' nest his fork had broken into. 'What am I to do with these fellows?' he said.

Hundreds of small orange ants in a frenzy of activity were carrying white eggs bigger than themselves away from a tumbled mountain of black earth clods, though quite where seemed uncertain for they were scuttling in all directions.

Some days earlier, Jac had come upon ants as he dug in

the patch Dada had declared was his, where he could plant flower seeds. 'Give your mother a nice surprise,' his father had said, handing over the packet. 'These are her favourites, night-scented stocks. Ask Dic to help you do it properly.'

Dic had shown him how to dig with his trowel, then break and rake the lumpy soil with a small garden fork until it was fine enough to sow the seed, and so all had gone well with his task until an ant appeared, a tiny thing. Orange. He dug in his trowel and covered it with soil. Moments later it reappeared – with a friend – and both scurried towards him. He hit them with the trowel and they disappeared, and in another moment they were there again, rather closer than before. He decided to move and knelt to dig and fork on the other side of his patch. He was busy and absorbed until he felt a sharp pinprick just above his sagging long sock. He looked and there were three little orange ants busily exploring his bare leg, and then another sharp pinprick. He got up quickly, brushing them off, scattered his seeds over the patch and hurried indoors to wash his hands.

His mother had looked up, surprised. 'Have you finished your gardening already?'

'Yes.'

'Put the seeds in?'

'Yes – and I got bitten by an ant.' But when he went to show where, below his knee, there was no mark and only a vague itch. 'It's better now.'

What Dic had uncovered in the clayey soil was an altogether grander ant city with winding, intersecting tunnels you could still make out in the larger lumps of soil.

'Somewhere in there,' he said, stirring the broken nest gently with the fork, 'is a queen, and she's bigger than the others, oh, five times bigger or more. And she lays all the eggs you see those tiny workers carrying about. They are trying to find somewhere safe to put them. Look how strong they are, moving the earth out of the way – and with those big eggs on their backs.'

'Strong as the spider in the wall?'

'Duw, yes! I think you're right. Perhaps stronger.'

'And are they as clever as the spider?'

'Now that's a good question. The spider, of course, is on her own, but here, in their nest, there must be hundreds of ants. Thousands! And they work together to make sure the queen gets the food she needs to lay all those eggs. You know, I used to work underground, as your father does now, and you have to plan so you can all work at the same time and don't get in one another's way. Well, these little fellows have their plans, and they work together just like I did with my butties, though I must admit they do seem to scramble on top of each other a bit.'

Left to themselves for a while, the ants seemed less frantic in their efforts and most were bearing their white packing cases in the same direction and gradually disappearing from the wreckage of the broken nest.

'They're clearing up nicely, don't you think?'

Jac nodded. 'They bite,' he said.

'Yes, indeed. You wouldn't want to get a few of them inside your shirt. But they are very clever. My old Dad told me that if you dug a little trench, with your trowel, across a nest, and filled it with water, like a river, so that some of the ants were on one side and some on the other … and if you put a couple of matchsticks …'

He paused to light his short pipe, have a puff or two and

shake the match out. 'And if you put the matches down on the ground so that the ants could see them ...'

He bent and placed the spent match where a few ants seemed to be looking for work. 'They would think a bit, then they would drag and push the matches across the river to make a bridge for them to cross from one side to the other without getting their feet wet.'

Jac and Dic stood together looking down. A few ants walked over or around the match, none showing the slightest interest in its potential as part of a building project.

'There's no water, see,' said Dic.

Jac was about to volunteer to get some from the kitchen when there was a thump and a brief metallic clatter from the other side of the garden. They both turned to see a strange boy of about Jac's age who, so far as they knew, might have fallen from the sky, lying on his back amid a litter of leaves and broken stalks in the rhubarb patch. A closer look revealed his descent had been accompanied by a large stone from the top of the wall separating the garden from next door's, and that the bottomless forcing bucket upturned on the rhubarb had been kicked aside.

'You all right, bach?' said Dic, striding over and helping the newcomer to his feet. 'What you doing in the rhubarb?'

Too shocked to cry, though his lower lip trembled, the boy rubbed his elbow and his shoulder, wiped his nose with the sleeve of his grey jumper and declared he was 'OK, I think.'

'Can't say the same for the rhubarb,' said Dic tidying the fractured stems and replacing the upturned bucket, 'but we'll see what we can save.'

Dinah, disturbed from her afternoon nap by the unusual noise, hoisted her fat, black body up the steps, ambled, bandy-legged, towards the little group and looked from one to the other.

'Look, she's smiling at me,' the boy said.

Jac was doubtful. 'Mm, I don't think so.'

'Don't touch her!' said Dic, alarmed. 'She'll go away in a minute.' And indeed she did, waddling off to a favourite spot, where she squatted, rose again and with a few nonchalant flicks of her back legs, scattered some earth on her latest deposit, before lolloping back down the steps and disappearing into the yard.

'Ah,' said Dic, with obvious relief, 'she's gone. Now let's see what we can do.'

With a grunt, he picked up the fallen stone and placed it on its broader edge in the gap at the top of the wall.

'You can't trust this old wall,' he said to the newcomer. 'Look by there – the mortar's like dust.' And, indeed, the purple mortar that bound the odd-shaped stones crumbled as he poked at it. 'So don't go climbing on it. Nor you,' he turned to Jac. 'You mightn't be so lucky next time a stone falls out.'

Jac had heard, without paying any attention, or having much interest in what was said, that George, the son of old Mr Roberts next door, who was a railway worker in Swindon, had come on a visit bringing his wife and young son with him. What he didn't know was that George had joined the army and, thinking the town where they were settled, a busy rail junction, was a likely target for air raids, had decided to move his family to his father's home in the relative safety of the valley. Now he looked at the stranger curiously and with a good deal of suspicion. He was somewhat taller and skinnier and his dark hair hung cropped in a fringe across his forehead, and he, too, had grey trousers, grey socks sagging below his knees, and black daps, the same as most boys.

'Well, what's your name, boi bach?' said Dic.

'Eric,' mumbled the boy, still somewhat out of sorts and looking at his toes.

'Eck?' said Dic.

'Eck?' said Jac.

'No, Er – ic.'

'This one's Jac,' said Dic, pointing to Jac, who was also looking at his toes. 'You're not going back over that wall. I'll let you out through the gate. Jac, let's see if the ants have moved that matchstick. Come on Eck, you too.'

They hadn't. The matchstick lay there still, and not a single ant was visible in the tumbled earth. But in this way introductions were completed and a friendship began.

*

A tentative knock at the front door sent Dinah into a paroxysm of fury. It was her invariable response to anyone who had the temerity to open the gate and approach the house. Most regular callers were used to it and stood their ground, but Eck was halfway down the path on his way out before Jo, with one hand firmly gripping the dog's collar, opened the door with the other.

'Did you want something?' she called after the retreating figure.

'Eh … is Jac coming out?'

'Who's asking?'

'Eric – Eck.'

Jo didn't answer; instead, without relaxing her hold while

Dinah still snarled and lunged at a visibly shaken boy, 'Jac,' she shouted, 'there's an Eric Eck wants you.'

Pausing only to ask his mother if he could go, and receive the usual plea to be careful, Jac put his wellies on and joined his new friend.

'That's a really nasty dog,' said Eck as they were walking up the street and around the corner to the black ash path at the back of the houses.

'She can be. Even bit me once.' Jac held out his hand, pointing to a tiny indentation on the palm. 'And she wasn't much more than a pup then. But she's a good guard dog.'

'What's she guarding?'

Jac thought for a moment, but there was no answer to the question. He shrugged.

'She's not like a normal spaniel. How did she get so fat?'

Not being familiar with spaniels as a breed, Jac was surprised. 'She's not fat,' he said, 'just a bit big – though she's always hungry. And she doesn't like people knocking the door.'

'Gave me quite a turn,' said Eck. 'H'm ... "The black-hearted fiend of the forgotten valley". Thought she fancied a slice of my leg.'

'What?'

'There's a stream up there,' said Eck pointing. 'I went exploring yesterday. Let's go and have a look.'

He was familiarising himself with his new surroundings and liked what he had found. The path skirted one of the old tips, in which finer rubble was mixed with larger blocks resembling nothing so much as dreadfully dog-eared stone books. With little effort you could split them into myriad misshapen grey leaves, on some of which were printed illustrations of ancient fern-like fronds. At the top of the path, the tip formed an amphitheatre overlooking a level patch on which stood Jac's father's shed and, opposite its doors, in a rushy dip, the few stark remains of the engine house, from which the upper courses of dressed stone and roof slates had long ago been stripped for re-use elsewhere. Within the mere stumps of the ruin, from which thick reinforcement bars protruded, the great iron drum of the winding wheel lay tilted on its axle, with room enough at its core for a small boy to crouch inside. Jac knew it all well.

'My Grancha says this place is haunted,' said Eck, relishing the idea.

'It's just bits of walls and a big old wheel.'

'It used to be a pit,' said Eck, 'so why is it like this? It's because of ghosts: "The Ghosts of the Pit".'

'I've never seen any ghosts – and I come here a lot, when my father's mending his bike.'

'But you don't come in the night, do you? The ghosts appear in the night. They're a miner and his son, just a boy, like about my age. You see them all pale and wavery, with their old lamps, sort of oozing up from under the ground.'

Jac looked around anxiously, although it was broad day, but darkening a little with clouds gathering over the mountain the other side of the valley.

'Why do you think they stopped digging the coal, leaving all these tips and things? It's because it's haunted, like I said. That boy and his father, a long time ago, were working in a deep tunnel under the ground – there's a level up there somewhere, all closed up with bricks now, I haven't found it yet – and they tapped a wall of coal with their picks and it gave way and a great flood of water came rushing in and drowned them. Drowned them both! Glug-glug-glug! Just up there.' He pointed vaguely towards the shaggy grass and bracken of the mountainside. 'Yes, closed up with bricks. I'm going to look for it.'

'I don't want to,' Jac said. 'Anyway, where did all the water go?'

'It's still there. A big lake, under the mountain – with skelintons ... skulls and bones floating around in the dark. And a brick wall holding it back. The ghosts don't mind, of course. They can get through brick walls.'

'Skelintons?' said Jac, blinking. 'I think I'll go home now. P'raps it's teatime.'

'Come on,' said Eck, leading the way to the wheel. He clambered up on it, saluted Jac from the top, and slid down the other side into rushes and oozing mud. 'Oh dear,' he said, looking at his shoes, muddied almost to the ankles, 'Well, I've done it now, might as well carry on. Let's make a dam.'

On the roughly levelled top of the tip, given time and tenacity, moss and grass and even occasional clumps of daisies and dandelions had established themselves, and there already was a pond thanks to the efforts of Sid Summers, who kept a flock of chickens nearby in low, pitch-coated sheds. Sid was lame, his chickens were his livelihood and, needing water for them, he had dammed the little brook that rose near the top of the mountain and cascaded steeply down through a Lilliputian chasm of blueish clay to within a few yards of their wire enclosure and black cots. It was not a large pond, just big enough for him to get a bucketful with a single dip, but as the years passed it had gathered a dense fringe of dark green rushes – and frogs, and frogspawn and tadpoles in their season and, even more fascinating, newts. Seeping from the pond, the brook trickled on a dozen yards or so to the edge of the tip, where it had carved a nick in the shale, and descended in miniature rapids and pools to the rushy bog surrounding the old engine house.

'Let's build our pond by 'ere,' said Eck, indicating a likely spot a short distance downstream of old Sid's. 'Look – we'll start with stones.'

He busied himself collecting odd lumps of shale and sandstone scattered about and, to Jac's amazement, stepped into the water to lay them across the bed of the little stream. The water spilled over the new obstacles in its path in a fine silver sheet.

'That's no good,' said Jac, 'it's all running out. But it's cleaned your shoes anyway.'

Eck standing in the flow, hands on hips, looked at Jac with eyebrows raised. 'That's just the start,' he said, with exaggerated patience. 'Now we need clodgins.'

'Clodgins?'

By way of explanation, Eck squelched to the edge of the tip where the thin green mat abruptly ended and, by alternately digging with the heel of his shoe and kicking at the shallow roots, dislodged a grassy clump.

'There you are – that's a clodgin. We'll need a few of those. Why don't you have a go?'

Willing though he was, Jac's efforts were futile: wellingtons were not designed for the job.

'All right, I'll dig 'em, you can put 'em on the dam,' Eck said, with obvious reluctance, 'so long as you're careful and do it properly.'

This seemed to Jac a fair and fitting division of labour. 'Yes, I've got wellies,' he said, wading into the stream.

Back at the construction site the water was clear – a brightly polished window through which every detail of the bed was visible. There, fragments of shale shone golden brown and silver grey, though if you dredged them up, they lost their bright, metallic sheen. Jac stood astride in the water, with sleeves pushed up, and placed the first clodgin with its thatch of grass adhering, like a green hedgehog, on top of Eck's foundation stones at the centre of the dam, where, in a few moments, it revealed a tendency to float away.

'I need more clodgins, quick,' he shouted.

Eck had returned to the edge of the tip and was gouging and kicking vigorously at the ground, but the clodgin remained rooted. With long grey socks sagging wetly around his ankles, head bent, black hair hanging lankly, nose dripping, he gathered his forces, kicked with greater vehemence and, much to his new friend's surprise, disappeared in a small cloud of grey dust.

Jac ran to the edge and was just in time to see Eck roll the last few feet to the bottom of the tip. Dust hung in the air and the path of his descent was clearly marked in the loose shale. The suddenness of his departure had been impressive; there was an almost heroic quality about the whole feat.

Jac hurried down the path and ran to his side. Razor-sharp fragments of shale had scored dozens of tiny lacerations in bare arms, hands and legs and he was sitting up watching specks of blood grow through a grey dust film into little red droplets. He looked at Jac, his face dark with grime except for two pale paths that meandered down his cheeks, gave his nose one long, slow wipe with the sleeve of his jumper from elbow to wrist, got up slowly, and without a word, still squelching, plodded off.

Jac picked up the clodgin, which had descended with his

wounded friend, returned to the new pond and put it in place. The water rose a little and pushed it off. It began to rain. He was grateful for the excuse to run home.

*

Jac already had two friends, Jimmy and Billy, who lived in one of the grey, roughcast houses across the road. They were brothers, but didn't look alike. Jimmy, the elder, taller, too, and thinner, had ginger hair and a narrow freckled face; Billy's hair was 'mousy' (Jo said) and his face, like his body, was pale, plump and round. Both were older than Jac, Jimmy, perhaps, older even than Eck. They were in the Boys' School, where Eck would join them. Jac knew nothing of the Boys' School, although its gate was no more than fifty yards from the Infants' he attended, beyond what he had learned from comics, that teachers were wrapped in floating black gowns, had funny flat hats and canes with crook handles that hung over a corner of the blackboard until brandished to punish talking in class or messy work, or anything really.

Comics had a big part to play in Jac's friendship with Jimmy and Billy – comics and the brothers' tent. One bright day early in the summer holidays, looking out of the front-room window, he saw the white tent on a patch of grass to the side of the Evans's house. He went outside to take a closer look because, though he knew at once what it was, he had never seen a real tent before. Curious, he crossed the road and was peering at it through the railings of the front garden when there was a muffled eruption of shouting from inside the tent and Billy crawled out. 'I'll tell Ma,' he threatened, sitting on the grass among the guy ropes.

Jimmy's head emerged from the tent flap. 'Oh, come on, don't be a baby,' he said. And then, noticing Jac outside, 'Want to see some comics?'

No reply was necessary. 'Close the gate behind you,' said Jimmy. 'We don't want sheep in.'

Billy had already resumed his place inside when Jac, on hands and knees, entered the sheltered space of filtered sunlight, no wider than his own small bed, supported by a pole at either end. A rough khaki blanket covered the grass. The brothers sat cross-legged, heads bowed over two piles of comics and between them lay Dash, their dog, a coarse-haired, black-and-white mongrel, part terrier and, remotely perhaps, part sheepdog. He was an old dog, but had a friendly disposition and was always eager to please. As Jac's face was invitingly low, he licked it.

'Ger off,' said Jac, without rancour, wiping the lick with his sleeve; then, seeing the comics, 'Where d'you get all those?'

'They're Freddy's mostly,' said Billy.

Freddy was their older brother who had left school at fourteen to work in the pit and, deciding at once he hated it, as soon as he was old enough, despite his mother's warnings, threats and pleas, joined the army. Never one for books, he enjoyed reading comics and regularly put aside a little of what he was allowed to keep of his weekly colliery pay packet to buy a bundle of them kept for him at the newsagent's. The *Hotspur*, the *Rover* and the *Wizard* had given him a taste for serial stories and, after reading, he kept each instalment carefully. Before he left, eventually to be a mechanic in the REME, Freddy had formally given his comics to Jimmy and Billy.

Jac was disappointed that many of the stories were told

in columns of print, not strips of cartoon pictures, like his favourite *Dandy*, but in the days and weeks that followed, sometimes, when the weather allowed, in the tent, sometimes under their mother's feet in the kitchen, he joined Jimmy and Billy poring over the pages. At first it took him a long time to read a single episode, but the stories were exciting and, with the example of the brothers before him, gradually he read more easily, eager to find what happened next.

On the last Sunday of the holiday, with school about to restart the next day, the three boys were gathered around a corner of the kitchen table reading and swapping comics, while Mrs Evans was busy in the scullery preparing vegetables for lunch and straining her ears to catch what was being said on the wireless. It was just after eleven o'clock. Suddenly she came into the room wiping her hands on her apron, saying, 'Hush, hush, I want to hear what's happening.' And so they all listened to the man say, 'This country is at war with Germany'. Mrs Evans bowed her head and raised the apron to cover her face, sobbing, 'Freddy, oh, Freddy.'

Soon afterwards, they heard the clack of the door latch and Mr Evans, who had been having his usual pint at the club up the road, came in, pale and open mouthed as though about to speak but saying nothing, until he drew a deep breath. 'Have you heard?' he said to his wife.

'Oh, Freddy,' she moaned, and he knew that she had.

'Why don't you boys go outside and play? Leave those old comics and have a breath of air. Go on.' And he switched off the wireless, stopping the voices, which had become a melancholy drone somewhere above and around them.

A momentary deep silence was broken by Jimmy's chair scraping back. He got up and, followed by Billy and Jac, left the kitchen and the scullery, redolent of roast, where untended saucepans were bubbling, and went out into the back yard.

There, too, all was still and quiet. It was Sunday: no shunting of coal-filled trucks on the railway at the foot of the Evans's garden, no movement of drams on the incline beyond, no cascading slag, no rattling of machinery from the screens. They stood, looking at one another, at the upper reaches of the green hillside across the valley, and the diagonal line of trees that edged the broad path climbing to the farms, the cloudy sky overhead.

'There's going to be a war,' said Jimmy. 'We're going to fight Germany. Freddy will be fighting, and we'll have to train ready, in case the Germans come here.' Then, thinking of what his older brother had told the family about his early weeks' experience in the army, 'We can do commando training up the mountain.'

'What's commando training?' said Jac.

'Freddy wrote to us, told us that new soldiers had to practise all sorts of things. Like running and wading through streams and dodging the enemy, and climbing up walls and things. And jumping down – and target practice with guns. We could train like that.'

This sounded a good idea, though Billy looked rather doubtful.

'I've got a cap gun,' said Jac. 'Can Eck come? He lives next door to us now.'

'Yes, so long as he can keep up.'

'When are we going to start?'

'After dinner.'

But they didn't. Jimmy and Billy went in, and Jac crossed the road to find his place ready at the kitchen table, Dada already carving the lamb and Mama filling the plates with potatoes and cabbage, slow curls of savoury vapour rising from meat and gravy.

'Where've you been?' said Jo. 'I called up the back, but you didn't answer.'

'I've been in the tent with Jimmy and Billy, reading comics. And there's going to be a war.'

His mother put down the saucepan with a clatter and his father looked grim. 'I don't think we want to talk about it,' he said. 'Let's be thankful for our food, and pray this war, if it's got to happen, is over soon, and not too many people get hurt. Not like last time.'

'Jimmy said we're going to practise being commandos.'

'I really don't want to hear any more about it,' Mama said, handing each plate in turn to Dada to add a slice of the roast.

'Can I go out after?'

There was no reply. And by the time they had finished eating and the plates were being cleared, it had begun to rain, quite heavily. Commando training was postponed.

*

The village had three collieries. Two near its steep end wall had vertical shafts penetrating deep underground and the pylon-like headgear with great wheels at the top by which men were lowered in cages to reach the coal-seam far below. At the third, a mere half-mile down the little river that divided one side of the valley from the other, miners reached their stalls, their work places, by a long, sloping tunnel running under the mountain. Jac's father worked in that colliery. He was the electrician and his work took him wherever, on the surface or underground, there were machines and lights worked by electricity. Among the machines underground were pumps that sucked-up and piped water away from where the colliers toiled at the coal face, for this was a 'wet pit' and, without them, it would quickly become a lifeless, drowned labyrinth.

It was Dic who told Jac about this, because his father never mentioned work at home. It was as though he had two quite separate lives, one preserved and cherished, which was home and family, and the other of shared danger and comradeship in a place of dank darkness, dust and noise, lit by the lamps of those who toiled there. Dic was always ready to interrupt his digging or planting or trimming to talk and draw husky breath. When Jac asked him about Eck's tale of ghosts in the old mine, which was too close to home, to his own bedroom, for him to be comfortable, the old man pushed back his cap, scratched his thin grey curls from habit, and smiled.

'Oh, well – his Grancha told him. I know his Grancha: he likes telling stories. Don't you go believing things like that,' he said wheezily, leaning on his shovel.

'But there was a pit up by the big wheel?'

'Duw, yes. You can still see the mess it's left, all that old shale. We've got pits all over the place; most of them finished working years and years ago. It must be riddled with holes down there, tunnels going everywhere and nowhere,' Dic said, pointing to the ground beneath their feet. And as soon as he had said it he was sorry, for he saw the boy's face cloud.

'Working underground can be dangerous sometimes, for all sorts of reasons,' he went on quickly, 'so we are very careful and we look out for our butties. My father told me that when he was young, working in another pit up the top of the valley, where they were sinking a shaft, one day the cage, oh, hundreds of feet down, was just being hauled up when it sort of slipped and got stuck in the shaft and the two men inside were thrown out into a great pool of water at the bottom.'

'And they drowned?'

'No. It was pitch-black down there – their lamps had gone out – and they were in this water, which was deep – oh, up to their chests.' He raised a hand to his chest to demonstrate. 'And in the darkness they felt about for a chain, which they knew was dangling down from the cage. Just think of them splashing around in the dark in that water, their clothes and boots getting heavier. But they found it. And didn't they hang on to that!'

'They hung on?'

'Oh, yes, indeed. But they were getting very tired. You know what it's like when your eyes want to close, so you can go to sleep.'

Jac, silent, troubled by the story, nodded.

'And one man, up on the surface, who saw something was wrong, went over to the top of the shaft and found out that his butties were down there hanging on, and he said let me go down with a rope and see if I can get them up. So they agreed and they had this long rope and they let him down on it – down, down into the dark.'

'But he couldn't find them.'

'Well, it wasn't easy. But he had a lamp, see. And there they were – still just managing to hang on to the chain. And the workers up-top lowered another rope and, one at a time, he tied it on to the poor colliers, soaking wet and so tired they were nearly letting go, and the men on the top pulled them up very carefully. And last of all the man who had rescued them.'

Jac, who had been holding his breath, now let it out in a long sigh. 'And they were saved?'

'Yes, boi bach, saved. Very, very sore from holding on all that time, and wet through and worn out, but not a scratch on them. And in an hour or so, they were right as rain.'

'Is rain right?'

'Do you know, I've never thought of that. But I suppose it must be.'

*

To begin with, commando training meant climbing up the steepest part of the mountain and running down. Jac soon found you cannot walk up a steep slope by simply putting one foot in front of the other, as you would climb steps. You had to turn your foot sideways and make sure it was firm in the grass before you raised the other foot to pass it. Jac's splay-footed progress was slow. Jimmy and Billy and Eck gave him a good start and he climbed as fast as he could, but quite soon he heard them breathing hard as they caught and then passed him. With their longer legs, Jimmy, Billy and Eck would always be quicker to reach the top, but they were patient with him and encouraged him: 'Come on, Jac – nearly there!'

He was a make-weight to be indulged, a responsibility to be looked after in whatever rough and ready way they were capable of, and at last, panting, he lay back on the grass beside them.

The steepness of the slope and shaggy, tufted growth of the grass didn't allow a sedate descent, rather it was accomplished, if at all, in leaps and bounds and with mind and body constantly alert and eyes fixed on the few rugged feet ahead.

The others launched themselves off the top with appropriate cries, 'Forward! Charge! Get'em men!' and apart from the odd spill, ran down full-pelt, though not with quite the élan Jo was mistress of. Jac's first attempt was far from sure-footed. He tumbled and rolled, but with cries of 'Come on, Jac!' now rising up the slope to him, he regained his feet and ran and jumped and ran again, and arrived in one piece, gasping and grinning, alongside the others at the bottom.

Climbing up was hard but, having succeeded in overcoming the temptation to descend backwards on all fours, running down was exhilarating. 'Let's do it again, is it?' he said.

Billy and Eck looked at Jimmy. Without discussion or vote, still less formal declaration, it was already acknowledged he was the leader. They were 'Jimmy's gang', and he had other ideas.

'We need target practice,' he said, and led them past the old winding wheel in its boggy patch to an ash-tip where, from time to time, people living in the street below had disposed of bucketfuls of cinders from their coal fires with other refuse. It was a spot favoured by the more adventurous of Sid Summers' chickens. Having squeezed through the fence around their cots, they would make their way down a worn path, pecking this way and that at whatever caught their beady eyes on the way to the midden. There, they would scratch a shallow depression in the ashes, wriggle themselves to a comfortable position in it and, head tucked under wing, doze contentedly. Perhaps instinct drove them. Or they just wanted to be alone. In any event, the clanking of old Sid's bucket as he limped up to bring their next meal would rouse them instantly and they would fly squawking back to their pen.

It was not roosting chickens that attracted Jimmy, but the

empty tins and jars and bottles lying among the ashes. The gang collected all they could easily lay hands on and carried their trophies to the big wheel's enclosure, where they balanced towers of tins on the broken walls and upturned jars and bottles on the stout iron reinforcements. A final few were left to decorate the upper parts of the wheel itself. It was a simple matter then to gather an ammunition store of conveniently sized stones on top of the bank of shale overlooking the targets on their firing range.

Lifting his lines from whatever period and theatre of war had figured in the films he had seen, or stories in his comics prompted, 'Load your weapons!' Jimmy shouted, and each member of the company picked a stone and weighed it in his hand.

'Take aim!' Arms were flexed and eyes fixed on tin tower, bottle or jar.

'Fire!' And a volley of stones rained down.

A cheer arose when a chance hit dislodged a number of tins that had been set close together, though it was impossible to tell who had been responsible for this success. Most of the hurled missiles had flown wide.

'Re-load! Aim! Fire!'

The sequence was repeated with similar unsatisfactory results. Jimmy surveyed the still standing tin towers, the untouched line of bottles and jars.

'Advance five paces. Fire at will!' he called.

The company slithered down the shale slope and, with a fresh supply of stones, proceeded to blast the enemy at point-blank range – about six feet or so, which even Jac found accommodating. As the array of tins toppled and bounced off their plinths with a sustained and satisfying clatter, he shouted

'Hurray!' and jumped in the air, his face flushed with exertion and pleasure.

The upturned jars and bottles, well separated on their iron stalks, provided stiffer resistance. Nothing less than a direct hit from a weapon of some weight would do, and eventually the mission fell to Eck and Jimmy. They proceeded to shatter them to flying jagged shards and splinters.

Jac would not have been able to say why he was excited by this short-range demolition of glassware, still less imagine how the airman felt watching the trail of destruction wrought by his bombs, but 'Shrapnel! Smithereens!' he shouted. There was something strangely satisfying – no, more than that, dangerously compelling in wanton destruction. When all of family and home had taught him to care for things, this was the opposite. He was thrilled by the sight and ringing sound of breaking glass, and the new words.

A single enemy outpost remained – the few targets precariously balanced on the circular rim of the big wheel.

'I've got a good idea,' said Eck. 'Somebody could go in the wheel while the rest of us knock the tins and bottles off – like sheltering from an air raid.'

'Or an artillery barrage,' said Jimmy, appropriating the plan. 'Who's going in? Billy, come on, you'll be all right in there.'

Jac thought, 'I could do that,' but hesitated to volunteer, and then Billy said, 'No fear! I'm not getting in the wheel while you throw stones at it. What if you don't aim straight? I'd catch it.'

'Go on. Baby!'

'Why don't *you* get in there and we'll throw stones?'

The act of insubordination cast a sudden silence like a

shadow across them, in which the clucking of hens was strangely audible.

Jimmy didn't answer the question. 'If you don't want to go in there, you might as well go home,' he said. 'You're spoiling everything.'

'OK,' said Billy, his cheeks burning. 'I've had enough anyway.' He turned and, viciously kicking a fallen tin out of his path, walked away.

The remainder of the troop looked at the retreating figure, and at one another, without sound or sign, then, 'Might as well finish them off,' said Eck, shrugging.

In a few moments he and Jimmy had despatched the remaining defenders of the bridge. They fell into the mud with hardly a murmur, giving their assailants no satisfaction. The game had lost its savour. They wandered back down the black ash path, said perfunctory good-byes first at Eck's back gate, then Jac's groaning portal. Jimmy, alone, trudged on, thinking 'You wait, Billy', but in the few minutes it took him to reach his own door the rancour had been largely forgotten.

\*

The valley, a 'dead end' or 'cul-de-sac', or 'box canyon' as black-hatted matinée rustlers might say, herding their stolen cows to a safe hideaway, was enclosed on three sides by mountains. Their Welsh names all included the word 'mynydd', which means 'mountain'. Outsiders might have protested that, with an altitude rarely much more than a thousand feet and the absence of rocky ruggedness, they hardly qualified for the term. Nevertheless, to everyone who lived there, mountains they were. Children played and, on occasion, grown-ups took walks 'up the mountain'. The highest point, Mynydd Disgwylfa, 'look-out mountain', an almost symmetrical tump, like a prehistoric barrow, from which the ancient people of the place might have observed Jo's advancing Roman invaders, was all of thirteen hundred feet. From this eminence, on a clear day, you might observe how valleys to east and west had gouged at the dank moorland with crooked fingers, and close by, in a boggy depression, near the heap of stones that were the remains of a cairn, the stream had its source. In spate, it was a bright quartz vein running down the darkest and steepest of the valley's slopes, but at the bottom it lost its momentum and mountain purity. Flowing at the foot of slag heaps, through air laden with shale and coal dust, it was black as the faces of miners emerging from the pit at the end of their shift.

Viewed from 'the other side', the profile of the mountain to the west of the stream was a spur sloping gently towards the south. Much of it was divided by hedgerows into fields, perhaps too steep to plough, that remained green and were sometimes dotted with sheep. The long diagonal of a broad path to the crest of the spur was marked by a row of trees lining its edge, and near the beginning of this path, on the slope below the trees, was a broad, maze-like patch of gorse, with individual thorny clumps five feet and more in height, and when the yellow flowers were in bloom, exuding a pleasant scent not unlike ice-cream. To the distant observer, the tree-lined path seemed to terminate at a stone-built, slate-roofed barn, but it continued around a bend between banks topped by strung wire or hawthorn hedges, and eventually fell away out of sight to a farm, and then on again to another farm and another valley.

Most of the mountain on the eastern side of the stream,

which rose steeply just beyond Jac's back garden gate, had neither fences nor hedges and was all shaggy grasses (some peculiarly blonde in summer) and dense bracken patches. Many of the paths that criss-crossed its slopes and summit had been deeply etched over decades by the to-ing and fro-ing of sheep, which seemed to prefer advancing, whatever direction they chose, in single file, creating narrow ruts along the hillsides' grassy flanks with the horny tips of their toes. The long rising diagonals of broader paths that led eventually over the top and into the next valley were man-made, offering to the able-bodied and sure-footed an alternative to a ten-mile journey by road. In earlier years, miners who had been sacked from local pits, or were for whatever reason unemployed, took this route to find work and, if they were lucky, trudged the same way daily, during winter months in pre-dawn and evening darkness.

Jo, out riding, explored the common paths and unfrequented ways all around the valley, often alone and in all weathers, content in her own company, trusting her pony and trusted in return. She discovered for herself the cairn below the look-out hill and, farther off, on an island of firm footing in the spongy upland, a long, low mound with an empty, stone-lined hollow sunk in the midst. 'For what?' she pondered, the charred bones once carefully deposited there having been scattered many centuries before.

On two legs of no great length, Jac's exploration of the valley expanded slowly, and very largely in the course of continuing military manoeuvres. On a fine Saturday afternoon in May, with Jimmy and Billy and Eck, and the brothers' dog, Dash, tongue lolling, tail wagging, an eager fifth member, he set out up the mountain. It was not long before the path became steeper and progress slower for all except the dog, which ran ahead and then hurried back to check everyone was following him.

'We'll cut straight up the mountain here,' said Jimmy, 'heading for the sandstone quarry. Forward-ho!'

His knowledge of the mountain had been gained with his older brother, whom he admired and thought of as an intrepid explorer. Freddy had told him to be wary of straying from established paths, and showed him as a warning, dangerously half-hidden in long grass, deep, narrow rocky clefts where the mountain seemed to have split its skin. It was Freddy, too, who had led him (as he told the others) to the highest point on the mountain, to a big, round pond, lonely and still, in a green saucer-like dip among the hills, and other special places that he would reveal in due course.

The lower slope of the mountain, not far beyond Jac's garden gate, had an open wound of reddish soil and rubble, perhaps created in a quest for building stone, perhaps the result of a landslip from nearby mining activity, but the sandstone quarry, further up the valley and higher on the mountain's side, was different. It was a small rock amphitheatre fronted by a smear of scree, like the track of a dark tear from a hollow eye. As they scrambled up beside the tip of small brown blocks and chips of stone, 'Plenty of ammo by 'ere,' Jimmy said – to himself it seemed, for no one had the inclination, or breath, to respond.

The quarry was a wonder to Jac. You entered over a lip of green into a shallow dip, wrapped around by the sides of the rocky arena, and picked your way over more rubble, more evidence of the work of masons shaping excavated rock with their chisels to a size and shape suitable for building. What had once been alive with the noise of hammering and gouging out with stout iron rods, and the voices of workmen, was strangely quiet. Even the steady breeze that, at this level on the mountain, persisted outside, constantly moving tufts of long grass this way and that, did not penetrate. There was only the sound of their breathing and the dog panting, and the pulse in their ears, until Dash, unnerved by the stillness, barked and broke the spell.

Jimmy surveyed his subdued troop with a look of triumph. 'It's great, i'n it?' he said, and picking up a conveniently axe-head shaped fragment knelt and bashed it against another stone, flat, like a thick slice of toasted brown bread, until it cracked and broke.

'See, by there – sandstone,' he said.

Fresh inside was the coarse dark orange sand of a primeval beach or seabed millions of years before.

'We need a look out,' he said. 'Who volunteers to climb to the top?'

Billy, Eck and Jac examined one another for a hint of eagerness, a scruple of courage. No one stepped forward.

'Come on, Eck,' said Jimmy.

'Ah – OK, I'll have a try. Where's the best place to start?'

Jimmy led them up a mound of moss covered earth and gravel to a point where the quarry face was somewhat lower, not as high as the roof of a house, but well up to a bedroom window, with a fringe of grass just visible at the top. The weathered rock was fractured vertically and horizontally and pitted here and there with shallow holes.

'Come on! Look,' he said, pointing, 'plenty of grips.'

Eck spat on his hands and rubbed them together, put his left toecap in one horizontal crack and the fingers of his right hand in another above his head and pulled himself up, leaving his right foot searching the air. 'I'm not used to this,' he said, half-turning his head, straining to see Jimmy standing behind him.

'Wait a minute … ' Jimmy grasped the heel of the dangling shoe and guided the foot to a hold. 'There you are.'

Billy and Jac had moved back from the quarry face and watched, transfixed, as Eck considered what to do next.

'Are you going to climb up?' Jac whispered.

'No fear!'

Jac was not familiar with the expression, but the tone of voice told him this was another situation in which Billy was prepared to rebel.

After an age of consideration, Eck raised his right hand to explore the rock face and, finding a hold a few inches higher, pulled himself up and successfully inserted the toecap of his left shoe into a quite spacious crack, which gave him a little confidence.

'I think I've got it,' he said, and by transferring weight and adjusting grip moved upwards until he was fully four feet above the ground. There, try as he might, fumbling the rock with fingers and feet, he could move no further.

Jimmy tried to be helpful. 'There's a crack just up on your right. No, not your foot, your hand. Your right hand. A bit along again. Not to your left. To your right. Don't you know your left from your right?'

It never took long for him to become exasperated. A minute later, standing legs apart, hands on hips looking up, he said, 'For goodness' sake, if you can't go up, come down.'

'No, I can't go any further up,' Eck said, and after a moment, ' – or down.'

'You've done it now,' said Billy, his voice betraying a note of satisfaction. 'He's stuck.'

Eck, spread-eagled against the rock, began to whimper. 'I'm stuck,' he said. 'I'm stuck. I can't get down.'

Jac's eyes were wide and bright. 'I can run down and fetch a policeman,' he said.

'I can't hold on much longer,' Eck wailed, 'my fingers are hurting – and my toes.'

Jimmy was not sympathetic. 'It's not far – just jump – or let go. We'll catch you. Billy, come and help.'

But unable to see how far the ground was beneath his feet, Eck was full of trepidation.

'He fell off our garden wall and hurt his elbow,' said Jac, ' – and fell down the tip.'

'Look,' said Jimmy, 'it's not far – I can hold your ankles.' And he did.

'Don't do that,' said Eck, 'I'll fall backwards.'

'Billy … Billy! Come and help!' Jimmy shouted.

Reluctantly, his brother joined him, both holding out their arms ready to cradle Eck's fall – just in time. He collapsed upon them and all three sprawled on the moss covered rubble.

'Oh! Ah!' said Eck, and then, 'That wasn't too bad. Not as bad as I expected.'

'It's all very well for you,' said Billy. 'I could have broken my arm … or my leg.'

Jimmy picked himself up and vented his frustration on Dash, who was running round them yapping with excitement, as if this unusual turn of events was for his benefit. 'Come here dog! Sit! Sit I said. Sit!'

Wagging his tail, the dog backed away to a respectful distance and sat, tongue lolling.

'Right,' Jimmy said, glad to have the episode over, even if it meant no one had been on look-out duty. 'We can't waste our time. Let's see how we manage under fire.'

The others looked at him. 'What do you mean?' said Billy. 'Who's the enemy? Where are they?'

'It's just a practice, isn't it?' said Jimmy. 'Jac can be on my side against you and Eck.' And, pointing to the quarry and stony terrain, 'There's tons of ammo here and plenty of cover.'

'I think its teatime,' said Eck.

'Only for a bit, before we go. It's practice! Look – you get well dug-in over there,' pointing to a succession of little dips and hillocks at the entrance to the quarry, 'and me and Jac will keep our heads down in a defensive position by 'ere, with our backs against the wall. And remember, we are not throwing *at* one another, just – sort of – near.'

Unconvinced, Eck and Billy nevertheless moved out, gathering suitable weaponry as they went, and crouched in a hollow, while Jimmy and Jac maintained their position under an overhang close to the quarry face.

'Everybody ready? Ready! Fire!'

All went well for a few minutes. Missiles flew through the air accompanied by suitable whistling noises, landing close, but not too close, to their targets.

All firing stopped at a plaintive 'Aw!' followed by a tearful whine.

Jac had been wounded. He had felt a sharp blow on the head and at the same moment heard, somehow inside, a distinct 'clonk' as though his skull was hollow.

Eck stood up waving his hands. 'I didn't aim at him – it was a ricochet.' (He pronounced the word, familiar from his reading of war and cowboy stories, to rhyme with 'Watch it'.) 'It hit the rock and bounced. It was a ricochet. Honest!'

Jac was holding his head and moaning and when he took his hand away and saw the blood he began crying in earnest. The other three gathered round the stricken figure as he rocked to and fro saying 'Oh my head is hurting. Oh, what will Mama say? I want to go home!' – the last a long wail.

'Let me see what you've done.' Jimmy's attempt at consoling was not entirely convincing.

'I didn't do it. It was him!' said Jac emphatically, between sobs, pointing at Eck.

'Just let me look – I won't touch it.' He pulled the hair gently aside. 'Well, it's only a little cut – on top of a little lump.'

'It's bleeding!' Jac began wailing again.

'Right,' said Jimmy. 'Get the medical man. Dash, Dash! Come boy.'

The dog, pleased to be in favour again, came to his side, tail wagging, alert for orders. Jimmy pointed to the wound and bloody, matted hair. 'There, boy.'

Dash (RAMC), needing no further instruction, applied a long, pink, wet tongue assiduously to cut and lump and the surrounding red stain until there was no sign of blood and, when the damp hair was allowed to fall back, you would never have thought anything untoward had occurred.

'If you don't tell, nobody will know you've had a cut. Isn't that right?' Jimmy looked round for support.

'Yes, that's right Jac. Nobody will know,' said Eck.

'Can't see a thing,' Billy added. 'Not a thing. Good as new.'

'Shall we carry the wounded off the battlefield?' said Jimmy.

'Yes, yes!'

They picked Jac up, and Jimmy and Eck, side by side, with arms crossed between, made a seat for him. And so he sat with his arms around their necks and they bore him away over a tump, and then Jimmy lost his footing on the uneven ground and they all collapsed together laughing. When they got to their feet, Jac was all right again, so they forgot about the battle and, Dash leading the way, tramped cheerfully home.

\*

Meanwhile, everyone was issued with an Identity Card, petrol rationing put a stop to occasional jaunts to seaside or country, and young men were called up for military service. Slung over their shoulders by a length of stout string, children carried cardboard boxes containing gas masks to and from school, where classroom windows were criss-crossed with brown sticky tape to mitigate the worst shattering effects of bomb blast. Daily papers reported the fall of Poland. Food was rationed. Everyone had a ration book. Germany invaded France, Belgium and Holland. Fascist Italy joined Germany to form the Rome-Berlin Axis. People were shocked to learn the fathers of families that kept Italian corner shops, who on Christmas Eves had thrown tangerines and handfuls of small coins to crowds of eager children, had been arrested and sent to an internment camp lest they take up arms against the villages which had been their homes for decades. Their wives, invariably addressed as 'Missis', took their places behind the counter and, though there was no more ice-cream, the shops stayed open, selling ever stranger brands of cigarettes, rationed sweets, cups of Oxo on chilly winter days and slices of Swiss roll at a penny each.

To Jac and most others of his age, the progress of the war was conveyed by cartoons. The caricatured, jack-booted villains were Hitler, a blustering maniac with black hair slicked across his forehead, toothbrush moustache and stiff arm raised in Nazi salute (also referred to, derisively, as Schicklgruber or, more commonly, 'Shit-legruber', quite why no one seemed to know, but it sounded appropriately unpleasant), fat Goering, with chestful of medals, and evil pipsqueak Goebbels. They were malign, vicious, implacably cruel killers and, at the same time, clowns, soon joined by the even more clownish, jowly Mussolini. The heroes were Churchill, always with a cigar and, in the years that followed, top-hatted, long, lean 'Uncle Sam' representing the USA, and a heavily-moustached, avuncular Stalin, alternating with a snarling bear, to stand for Russia. Billy became a great collector of cartoons. He scanned the daily newspaper for them and took pains to trace and transfer them to the blank pages of one of his father's old business ledgers. He did not gain a great deal from the political messages they contained, but learned how to draw in a way that excited admiration from other members of the gang, even his brother Jimmy. Words strange to tongue and lips – 'Blitzkrieg', 'Panzer', 'Luftwaffe', 'Gestapo', 'Swastika', 'Stuka', 'Heinkel', 'Messerschmitt' – were tried and added to conversations in school yards. News in the daily papers and the cinema graphically displayed the effects of heavy artillery and bombing raids that seemed to be getting ever closer: huge night fires and explosive destruction in towns and cities and, by dawn light, shattered and tottering skeletons of buildings, great piles of smoking rubble, firemen, ambulances. On land there were barrage balloons, ack-ack guns tilted at the sky, brave RAF fighter pilots racing to their Spitfires and Hurricanes, the twisted wreckage of German bombers and, at sea, speeding warships with waves breaking over their decks, or, torpedo-holed, sinking at the bow or stern, dazed, life-jacketed sailors looking up at their rescuers from crowded small boats. Images of war, impressed indelibly on everyone's mind, were a source of anguish to those who had a father, husband, son or brother involved in the fighting (you rarely knew where).

From time to time the penetrating, loud wail of the air-raid siren dipping and swelling warned of enemy aircraft approaching and people looked fearfully to the skies. But seeing nothing there, they soon carried on with whatever they were doing. Still it was a relief when the siren howled again a sustained long note announcing the all-clear. Bombs fell elsewhere, once on another mining village not far off, where houses were destroyed and people killed, but the mere crease in the hills that was Jac's home seemed blessedly insignificant to raiders and bomb-aimers. On rare occasions the slow throbbing drone of a German plane would cross the blackout night, and those who heard it held their breath until the sound faded. It was bound elsewhere, or perhaps lost. An air-raid shelter, built of brick, windowless, with an enormously thick, concrete flat-roof, appeared, as if by magic, fifty yards from Jac's house. The only shelter in the valley, it had a slatted wooden door secured by an ostentatiously large padlock. Jac peered through the slats into the dark interior and sniffed its stale, mouldy air, but quite soon it ceased to be of any interest, an inert, ugly, disregarded thing destined never to be used.

And then, in the depths of thick night, early in the new year, without the faintest siren warning or anyone heeding, high up, the aircraft's pulsing hum, a bomb tumbled out of the sky into the valley. It struck a boggy patch of mountain, all dark green moss and rushes with water seeping, just behind the church, a mere skip and a jump from the road ascending the valley, its terraced houses and sleeping people. Perhaps the explosion was muffled by the spongy terrain; certainly Jac and Jo and their parents, no more than a couple of hundred yards away, heard nothing. The news was brought by an early caller, just after Dada had got the fire going on that Sunday morning, and he roused the family to tell them that the war, which was on all minds, but had been going on in other places, had finally reached them.

Jac dressed hurriedly and was ready to go at once to see what had happened. He was told to be a good boy and eat his breakfast and, after he had gulped it down, to dress properly and warmly, because it was cold and damp outside.

He found himself joining a steady stream of the curious hurrying up the rough, unsurfaced road behind a long terrace towards the church and then, in pale morning light, cutting up the slope behind, where a crowd was gathered in a circle on top of a heap of reddish clay. That, Jac knew at once, was not as it had been before, because he was familiar with this oozing place, where you might be fortunate enough to come upon a frog that would spare a momentary glance of its bulging eyes before leaping out of sight into the morass of moss and rushes. He squeezed his way through the crowd to the top of the mucky heap and looked down into a bomb crater, fully twenty feet across, like an inverted, reddish cone sunk into the slope, with wisps of smoke rising from its depths, as though a volcano had turned itself inside out.

A shout, 'Jac! Jac!' a little distance off around the circle of gaping observers drew his attention.

It was Eck, waving excitedly. 'Come and see what I've found.'

It took a little time to extricate himself from the crowd,

slither down the erupted pile of mud and clamber up again to his friend's side.

'Look,' Eck said, revealing in his gloved hand a slightly curved jagged shard of metal, with torn bright silver edges. 'It's part of the bomb. Don't touch! It's still hot.'

It was indeed, though not hot enough to burn. Jac was entranced. 'Where'd you get it?'

'Just by 'ere. I trod on it – in the mud.'

Jac looked at the ruddy clag around his feet. By this time other boys, some newly arrived from further parts of the valley were scouring the churned ground – and one or two shouting excitedly. Jac was resentful of their success, resentful of their presence at the crater. 'Let them wait for their own bomb,' he thought, and he began to dig with his heel in the sticky surface and gouge with his toe. No fragments of bomb emerged. His black boots were liberally smeared and he was taller by an accumulated inch of muck on the soles.

With a note of triumph, Eck said, 'Look – I've found another piece!'

He had, indeed. It was smaller than the one he had stowed in his pocket, but it was from the bomb and had the same appearance of strangely solidified forked lightning.

'It's shrapnel,' he said and they looked and poked at it together. 'It'll look great when it's been washed a bit, you'll see. There – you can have it.' And he handed it to Jac, who stood open-mouthed with shocked gratitude, and was immediately anxious to go home and show his prize.

Older spectators, having seen what there was to see, were moving off down the slope and away, wiping footwear on the damp grass as they did so. Some boys, late arrivals, but full of hope, were searching the mud, a few slipping and sliding down the steep sides of the crater, which still exhaled occasional spirals of smoke, as though someone was having a cigarette in the depths.

It was a gloomy day, the sky sombrely cloud-covered as they turned aside from the crater. 'The church was hit too,' said Eck. 'Let's have a look before we go home.'

At first Jac couldn't see any change in the building. From the mountain slope, just above it, the roof appeared intact, two bells still hung in the arched stone turret at the further gable end.

Eck pointed: 'The windows have gone.'

Jac saw then that the entire large window, frame and stained glass, that faced the mountain was a dark empty space and the two smaller windows on the nearer side wall were shattered. 'The roof doesn't look right either,' he said. 'It's shifted a bit.'

'The explosion must have done it. Boof!' said Eck, throwing his arms up dramatically.

They had walked only a few yards along the rough road towards home, when Jac noticed a small window-sized gap at ground level in the high wall beside them. It was the familiar sort of access to household coal stores in some of the terraces. When a fresh load was delivered to the lane outside, it was a simple and speedy matter to open the wooden door and shovel the coal in. But there were no coal deliveries on Sundays.

'That door must have been blown in, too,' said Eck.

Jac bent to look inside. 'It's not a coal-cwtch. It's got big glass jars in.'

The increasing light of a winter sun emerging from cloud over the mountain to the east revealed a tidy row of large, stoppered jars, faintly blue and brown and, around them, scattered packages.

'What's all those?' he said. And, as Eck bent to look, 'I know – it's the doctor's house. They must be his medicines.'

What neither could see behind the wall (though they heard about it later) was that one side of the roof of the house beyond had been stripped of its slates, which had showered into the garden and spun away dangerously down the road in front. If they had thought about this freakish outcome, it would have taught them a little about the unpredictable, weird effects of bomb blast.

Water soon gathered at the bottom of the bomb crater, a single eye gazing at the sky out of a deep, red socket. In the weeks that followed, sometimes on his own, sometimes with friends, Jac walked the same road past the doctor's damaged house. On these occasions he always peered in at the cellar store to view the great coloured jars. It was many weeks before a new door was fitted, and many years before the church windows were replaced and the shifted roof made safe. There were other priorities in wartime.

The jagged fragment of shrapnel Eck had given Jac found a place on the stone sill outside the kitchen window, occasionally sharing the space with a jam jar movingly speckled with tadpoles, which was far more interesting than a piece of twisted metal. It rusted and eventually disappeared. Jac didn't miss it and never asked where it might have gone. Within a few days, all who were interested and could be bothered had seen the roughly sculpted addition to the shape of the valley and had no desire to see it again. Left to its own devices, the sodden terrain of the lower mountain slope where the bomb had fallen set about restoring itself. Slowly, but very surely, the red mud crept forward to fill the crater, while mosses, grass and rushes spread their seeds and advanced to heal the wound.

*

Jo and Jac's father knew as much about horses as he did about motorbikes. He had been brought up with them. When he was a boy, transport of all kinds and for all purposes often made use of live horse power. Even now, every day underground he shared the available space (and there was sometimes very little) with horses. In the years before the war, the clopping of hooves was a familiar sound on the road that looped around the valley, for fruit and vegetables were sold from one horse-drawn flat cart, fresh fish and cockles by the quart in their shells from another. A rag-and-bone man regularly toured the side streets with his scruffy nag and gargling cry, 'Rags-bones! Rags-bones!' In summer, at weekends and on sunny evenings, the Italian corner shop's decorated cart would sell ice-cream, pink and white, from a pair of chilled silver drums, in cornets and wafers or scoops in your own dish. And even during the war milk was dispensed from a grand cream-coloured, caravan-like dray pulled by a docile shire horse that knew every stop on the round.

As Dada said, there was much more to having a horse than riding it, but Jo had not been put off by the promise of hard work. Her first was a small bay with black mane and tail that seemed the right size for her, and Bonny, for that was the pony's name, served her well. A large hotel dating from the early coal-rush days, which had not welcomed a guest since it was briefly occupied by a squadron of Huzzars brought in to quell rioting strikers almost forty years before, had stabling for six horses across a steep, cobbled lane, similarly unoccupied since the soldiery had left. It was glad to provide a stall at a modest rent. Only a short distance up the road from home, with a piped water supply, electricity for lighting, and a narrow yard where swept straw and manure could be piled until well aged and ready to distribute to keen gardeners, it was ideal. Bonny was the only occupant. This was convenient, because there was plenty of room to store bales of hay and straw, large sacks of chaff and smaller sacks of oats, for bedding and feed, and the odd misshapen block of rock salt for licking. The pony may have been lonely, for whenever Jo or Dada approached and unlocked the door, she would whinny – with pleasure, Jo said, at the promise of a little human company. Remarking the pony's portly bearing, Jac thought it was the prospect of having her manger refilled that stimulated the greeting.

Another duty was added to their father's morning routine. Having lit the kitchen fire, taken Mama a cup of tea, and had a bite to eat himself, he now went up the stable to see that all was well there before going to work. It meant rising even earlier. Jo, too, had to set her loud-ticking alarm-clock to ensure she was up to attend to Bonny's needs, which she did, before her own, and regardless of the weather. A pony was a responsibility.

Jac became used to helping out at weekends and during school holidays by brushing the grey-pavioured floor of the stall with a stiff cane broom, sweeping the soiled, sweet-smelling heap of straw and droppings out to add to the pile in the yard, and then laying down fresh straw. When Jo did this, she would slap the pony's rump with a firm, 'Get over', and Bonny would move to one side without demur to allow the brush easy access to all parts of the stall. Jac, who found it difficult to replicate the indelicate slap and summon up the peremptory tone of command, was reduced to sweeping around the pony's hooves and under her belly. Bonny, her head deep in the manger, would stop mid-munch, look back, revealing the white of her eye, and move slyly towards him until he was pinned, helpless, against the tall wooden partition. The pony was getting on in years and well aware of what she was doing. Jo told him it was her idea of a joke, and Jac felt a little humiliated, though not resentful. Other jobs were beyond him. He might fill Bonny's bucket with water, but was neither tall nor strong enough to lift and place it in its compartment in the manger. If thirsty, she would push him out of the way with her head, quite gently, and syphon up the contents as it stood on the floor.

Jo had grown, not a great deal, but enough to lend weight to her appeal for a bigger pony, and when she left school and gained employment as a shop assistant in the local Co-op store, Dada agreed to find one for her. So Betsy, a pretty chestnut mare with a white blaze down her face and white socks, was introduced to the stall next to Bonny's. It had been the intention to sell the little bay, but just then no one was interested enough to buy. Since Betsy arrived with her own tack, both horses were equipped for riding and, as both needed exercise, it seemed the right time to encourage Jac to ride.

Part of him liked the idea. He could see himself riding, one with the pony, encountering friends, raising his crop in passing salute, sharply nudging the horse's ribs with his heels, urging her to a canter and leaving them enviously watching his receding back. He admired the way film cowboys rode, upright in the saddle with such easy control, almost as though they were seated in an armchair, except for the blur of the hooves beneath. There was something heroic about the horseback posture of even the black-stetsoned rustlers and renegades. That was how he would have liked to appear to the valley's pedestrian population, but the more time he spent in the stable with Bonny and Betsy the less confident he was of his ability to control them.

With Jo's encouragement he determined to try. He had seen his sister slip on Bonny's bridle and bit a hundred times, seen her lift and place the saddle on the pony's broad back and tighten the girth to hold it securely in place, seen her, with a word and twitch of the reins, guide her mount out of the door to clatter down the steep cobbles, where often she slithered and sometimes her shod hooves struck sparks.

When the time came, while he struggled to copy his sister's deft handling of horse and tack, Jo held the pony's head and talked soothingly to her. All went well enough until it came to putting on the saddle.

'Make sure the girth is tight.'

'I am making sure,' said Jac, hauling at the strap, while Bonny fidgeted. 'That's it.'

'Right then, let's see how you mount up. Foot in the stirrup. Not that foot. You'll be facing her tail!'

Hiding a blush, Jac changed feet, put his weight on the stirrup to pull himself up and fell under the pony's belly as the saddle slid down and around.

'I thought you said you'd tightened the girth.'

'I did. I did!'

'Not enough,' said Jo. 'Mind you, she's clever. I'm sure she takes a big breath and holds it as you start tightening so that you think the strap has gone as far as it will go – and then she breathes out.'

'That's not fair!' said Jac.

'No, but I bet it gives her a laugh.' And as Bonny looked round at them, showing again the white of her eye, 'Come on, I'll have a go at it.'

Jo swung the saddle round onto the pony's back and examined the still buckled strap.

'Look,' she said, 'it's two notches short of the usual place. You can tell from that dark line on the leather. That's how far you need to pull when you tighten it.'

It was another lesson to add to those Jac had learned about feeding, watering and grooming a horse, and sweeping a stable, none of which he had found easy, largely because he lacked that empathy with horses which had come so readily to his sister. To him, even a small pony like Bonny was a large and wilful creature, which if the choice was his alone he would have nothing to do with. But at last, with his sister's help, he began to ride. Their early outings were brief. They led the horses up the cobbled lane to the quiet, unmade road behind the terrace, mounted there and ambled quietly up to the bomb-blasted church and then down to the back gate of the house, where Jo would lightly dismount, tie Betsy's reins to the gatepost and fetch their mother to see Jac on his pony. Mama would say how fine he looked in the saddle, and to take care.

Back at the stable, brother and sister together would remove saddles and bridles, see the horses had feed and water and hay in the rack for the night, give them a final pat, and switch off the light, because even in summer only a little daylight penetrated the stable from a transom window, and lock up. Those final moments, listening to the tranquil munching of the horses, Jac began to enjoy. He found in them a satisfying warmth, mingled with relief that their outing together had passed with no mishap.

Gradually the rides extended to the familiar broad paths up the mountain; gradually Jac began to feel a little more at ease on horseback. And there was one fine summer day when they rode over the crest of the ridge and dismounted for a while and sat on the grass keeping a light hold on the reins while the ponies, chestnut and bay, glowing in the sunlight, arched their graceful necks and sucked water from a lonely pond. Nothing was said, but Jac had never felt closer to his sister, there in that quiet, empty place among rolling hills, with the still water reflecting blue sky and white cloudlets, the distant faint music of a skylark's song, and the companionable horses now cropping the grass, all in their own way contented. He thought suddenly of the romance of the West, cowboys and the enormous prairie stretching away on all sides beneath an endless sky, and felt a momentary quiet delight surge through him.

With such experiences, Jac was close to discovering pleasure in riding and a love of horses that his greater ease with them gave him. Although she didn't say so, Jo sensed this and was pleased for him. She spoke of longer rides they might take together to the hill farms the other side of the valley. It was a route familiar to her: she and her pony were well enough known to be greeted as friends by the sheepdogs and farm workers, when most people were considered unwanted intruders and met with choruses of shouts and barking.

She and Jac had led their ponies down the cobbled lane to the main road on several occasions and mounted there to ride at a decorous walking pace, the ponies' shod hooves clattering on the tarmac in a syncopated rhythm. Jac sat as straight in the saddle as he could make himself, conscious of the eyes upon them as they passed by houses and shops, that he was being seen, if not watched. There were few motor vehicles to be wary of and, if a bus appeared, Jo had told him to fall behind and follow her until the noisy distraction had passed. All had gone well, and on a summer Saturday late afternoon, Jo home from work, the weather fair, they pointed the ponies down the road, turned right at the corner shop, where the Co-op stood opposite, passed the Workmen's Hall and crossed the bridge over the railway. Below them, out of sight, lines of coal trucks waited to be filled, but there was no steam engine and no sounds of activity rose from the screens. They paced quietly along the straight stretch of road built upon the old tip of pit waste, around the railings enclosing the park, where children were chasing one another, their voices loud, past the concrete sheep dip and onto the path to the farms.

Whatever its remoter origins, the path, slanting diagonally up to the crest, had been widened by digging into the hill and piling the reddish, stony soil into a retaining bank on the other side. Ash from the engine houses of the collieries, of which there was a plentiful supply, had been spread over the bare earth and tamped or rolled to provide a firm and lasting surface. The roots of trees planted on top of the bank held it firmly, so that there was no danger of the structure and the ash road itself being washed away down the steep hillside. All that had happened long before Jo and Jac rode up the hill beneath the leafy canopy of branches spread from trees already tall.

They met occasional walkers strolling along the path, some with dogs. Jac noticed a change in the rhythm of Bonny's movement whenever a dog stood and sniffed in her direction, but she settled as soon as the dog moved away.

'I don't think she likes dogs,' Jac said.

'It's the same with most horses. You'll get used to it. Don't show her you're afraid.'

'But I'm not afraid of dogs.'

'You mustn't show her that you're afraid she doesn't like dogs.'

'How do I do that? Do I tell her?'

Lacking an answer, 'Oh, just keep going,' his sister said.

Part of the black path was already in the hill's shadow and the afternoon sunlight, filtered through leaves, made a lacy dappled border of its further edge and the green bank. At the top of the hill, where the lane swung right, the old stone-built barn stood still in full sun. They had outpaced the straggling walkers. Opposite the barn, the other side of the lane, the hill, patched with bracken, rose gently. Jo dismounted and led the chestnut to the grassed slope.

'A little rest before we go back,' she said, and sat down, the reins looped around her wrist, looking thoughtful.

In a moment Jac had joined her. 'What's the matter Jo?'

'I'm not sure how many more outings like this we'll be able to have. How much time I'll be able to give to the horses.'

Jac was silent, not knowing what to think. At last, 'You're not going away?' he said.

They were sitting close together looking across to the other side of the valley, their side, steeped for this time in its own sun, the mountain dotted with sheep, the lines of low, broken walls running down the hill like grey tears.

'No, not away, I hope. But I'm going to have to give up my job in the shop, because I'm eighteen and parliament in London says I've got to do something to help the war effort. So you'll have to go riding by yourself. Perhaps you can exercise Betsy as well. Two horses – they'll keep you busy!'

She smiled to see Jac's perplexed frown. 'And there'll be more work to do in the stable – you'll enjoy that.' She laughed, and they laughed together. 'Come on,' she said, 'let's forget those things for a bit. I could do with a cup of tea.'

They pulled up the horses from their contented grazing and returned to the path, Jo noticing, with satisfaction, that Jac was no longer clumsy getting on a horse. 'You'll be all right,' she said, half to herself, as she took her place on Betsy. The walk back down the path, past the sheep dip and along the road by the park was as pleasant as any Jac had experienced on Bonny. He and Jo spoke little, but there seemed to be a quiet understanding between them, and a mutual affection beginning to overcome their difference in age.

As they were turning right at the beginning of the road running straight to their side of the valley, there were again the sounds of children playing in the lane at the back of the terraced houses. The shouts and shrieks grew louder and suddenly a gang of small boys and girls burst into the open and came running towards the road. Bonny, startled, threw up her head, but what followed was far more disturbing. A bigger boy swishing a long, thin stick came running around the corner, a small black dog bounding and barking at his heels. Both horses skittered, their hooves clattering on the road, and Jo, struggling to hold Betsy, had no time to do or say anything, before Bonny, snorting with fear, took flight.

Jac had barely experienced trotting, far less a canter on horseback, and the little bay set off at full gallop. His only instinct was to hang on, crouched low, to the tangle of reins and long black mane as the pony raced along the straight, over the bridge above the railway, past the cinema, up the short slope between the corner shops to the road junction and straight towards the Co-op store. The last yards uphill had finally exhausted her when a night-shift collier on an afternoon stroll caught her bridle and stopped her inches from the shop window.

By the time Jac returned fully to his senses, Jo had come up. When Bonny bolted there had been no time to think or feel anything, but now she was appalled at what might have happened if he had fallen on the unyielding gravelled surface of the road, and almost wept with relief to find him in one piece.

'You all right, boy bach?' said the collier.

'Oh, thank you – thank you very much. I think he's all right,' said Jo, while Jac sat still in the saddle, incapable of words, and the two horses, nostrils redly flared, stood trembling.

'We'll be all right now. Thank you. Thank you. She might have gone through the window.'

'Don't think she could have managed it,' said the collier. 'She'd only have bashed her nose. She's blown. Run out of puff! Anyway, all's well.' And, smiling, he continued his way down the road.

By the time Jo and Jac, who was still shocked and silent, had led the horses back to the stable and rubbed them down, and fed and watered them, the story of the bolting pony had spread.

Mama was waiting anxiously and, full of concern, greeted them as they came in through the back door.

'Are you hurt?'

'No, no – he didn't get thrown off,' said Jo. 'At full gallop! – all the way across.'

Tongue released at last, and with a burgeoning awareness that his desperate ride might be viewed as an achievement, 'Nearly ended up in the Co-op window,' Jac said. 'Smash, bang in the middle of the new shoes.'

'A man stopped her,' said Jo. 'He told me she didn't have the breath to go further. Worn out she was by then.'

'I can't bear to think of it,' said their mother, 'and I won't hear any more. I don't want you riding on the roads – it's too dangerous.'

Nothing more was said in the house. Bonny was sold soon afterwards, before Jac had the chance to ride her again, even if he had wanted to, which (without admitting it to anyone) he was very uncertain about. Within the month, Jo had a new job in a munitions factory. The young men, as they now were, she had once ridden with were in the Forces, or worked shifts in the colliery, while her own working hours, lengthened by travelling, gave her fewer opportunities to ride, though she seized every one. She and Betsy trekked the mountain paths alone, and her love of riding, for the release it gave from a more arduous, and dangerous, working life, continued to grow.

*

Almost as in primitive times, whatever the season, but most of all in winter, the kitchen fire was the centre of the home. Its warmth and light were salve to the spirit for everyone in the valley. Most fires were allowed to burn themselves out overnight, and the first task of day was to rattle grey cinders with the poker, scrape-shovel fallen ashes into a bucket to take out, and lay the fire afresh. Although he was too young to share in the activity, Jac was familiar with all that needed to be done. Sheets of yesterday's newspaper, roughly twisted, made the bed on which dry sticks were laid and, once some coals had been placed carefully on the sticks, the match put to the paper usually also lit his father's first cigarette of the day. Another double-page broadsheet spread of news stretched from hob to hob would suck in the draught that brought pale wood to brief but vivid life, transformed coal-black to glowing red and set the refilled kettle singing again.

Like the coal, the sticks, too, came from the pit, carried home by colliers: two short, stout cylinders of pit prop timber tucked under the arms, ready for chopping and drying. Jac had watched his father chopping sticks, on one knee in the back yard outside the coalhouse. He raised the small, sharp axe and brought it down smartly with a smack on the wooden block before him, chopping it in two and, without seeming to take aim, smack, smack, smack, he deftly split each part in turn into piles of creamy yellow sticks while the faint scent of resinous pine rose about him.

A sharp shower brought Jac running to the house. At the end of lessons, he had set out from the school gates enjoying a meandering, joshing stroll with friends, and then as the sky darkened from the west and rain began to fall stringing a tributary cleft of the valley like a hushed harp, they scattered, heading for the nearest way home. He found his father, not long come in from work and still in his pit clothes, coping with a ton of coal dumped by the usual lorry outside the back gate. Dada had just rolled up his sleeves and was surveying the load when the first drops fell. The coal lay before him in a heap like a smashed black pyramid, dully glistening. There were big, jagged lumps, pick-faceted, almost crystalline, as though instinct with the deep thought of diamond in their carbon hearts, a rubble of sizeable lumps like polished hand axes, a spreading delta of gravelly small coal, and dust, black dust, already with the rain beginning to lose itself in the ashy surface where it lay.

The load had to be carried down the clumsily cobbled garden path and three steps to the doorless opening of the coalhouse in the back yard, and there was no point in waiting and hoping for the shower to pass. As Jac, head hunched into shoulders, darted by him with an unnecessary shout, 'It's raining!', Dada was bending to pick the largest lump up from the heap and carry it in his arms down path and steps and into semi-darkness under the pattering tattoo of rain on corrugated roofing to begin a foundation layer where he had already brushed back the remains of the previous load. One or two at a time other big lumps followed as, with hair a slicked silver helmet close to his skull, he tramped up and down until he had built a wall, almost waist high, across the roughly paved floor. Then, in bucketfuls, pitched behind the black barricade, came the lesser lumps, and after them the small coal and finally the shovelled mass of all that could be recovered of the rest of the load. He didn't pause to survey the finished job, which in the dim light resembled nothing so much as a coal seam recreated. Having made sure all was swept tidy and filled a bucket with coal for the evening fires, dripping wet with rain and sweat, he stepped across the yard and opened the door to the warmth of the back kitchen.

'You're soaked,' Ede said. 'Why don't you have a quick bath before you eat?'

'I suppose I might as well. It would rain! Ah well.'

He sat on the fender in the glow of the fire and untied his pit boots. Before he had taken them off a mist was rising from his shirt on the side close to the bars of the grate.

'Bring those things down for me to dry properly.'

'They'll be all right if I hang them up.'

'No they won't,' she said.

He smiled wryly and padded away up the stairs.

When he returned, face shining from the bath, Ede, with a grimace, took the damp, pit-stained clothes from him and spread them on chair backs one side of the fire, where most of the stench of steaming wool and coal-must was drawn up the chimney. She quickly washed her hands, and with a tea towel to protect her fingers, brought his dinner, kept warm on top of the oven, to the table. Without a word, he sat and ate with gusto, and sipped his black tea, a habit of the pit, because it was what filled the tin jack he carried to work daily to slake his thirst and lay the black dust he breathed.

Jac was finishing the toast he had made himself, holding a slice of bread before the bars of the grate with the long-handled fork Uncle Percy had fashioned from copper in the colliery blacksmiths' shop. Toast and jam, this time strawberry, was a tea-time favourite. Best of all was wimberry jam. Its flavour could stir memories of the wimberry patch up the mountain that Jo, who discovered it out riding, had warned him to tell no one about or it would be scrumped before they had taken their share. They had gone there early in August with two big tins and filled both with plump blue-black berries, though Jo had done much the greater share of picking, kneeling, then half-lying, close to the ground among the low, coarse clumps of wimberry bushes, while Jac plucked some that rattled at the bottom of his tin, ate some, added a few more to his store, and sat and gazed about him at the mountain and the grazing sheep, and the plumes of white smoke that climbed from the collieries in the valley below. And when they brought their harvest home, Mama said the berries looked wonderful, quite the best she had seen, and how hard they must have worked to pick all that many (at which Jac felt guilty), and she would make a tart with them. As it turned out, there were plenty for two fine tarts, and enough left over, including smaller, somewhat paler fruit, mostly from Jac's less discriminate picking, to make a jar of jam that, for a while, preserved a subtle perfume of summer into a rumbustiously stormy autumn.

The kitchen, hub of the house, was simply furnished. It had a scrubbed deal-plank table and wooden chairs, and a glazed brown Belfast sink with brass taps, hot and cold. Below the fireplace, with its two brick pillars black-leaded to a glow and stout iron bars fronting the basket, was a bright brass stand, where saucepans could be left to simmer, astride the patterned steel fender. A cluster of fire irons together with the long toasting fork leaned against the polished wall on one side and a big oven was built into the other. This fire was the main source of warmth in the small universe of home: it heated the water; it was where everything that needed cooking was brought; around it the family gathered, talking or listening to the wireless; it was where they ate. The oven was also where sticks to light the fire were thoroughly dried before they took their place in a neat stack on the top, ready for the morrow. Before and even at the beginning of the war, when it was still possible to buy meat directly from pig-keepers, a well-salted piece of pork belly hung from a big hook in the ceiling to be sliced for breakfast, when the perfume of its frying filled the house. It was always warm in the kitchen, because there was always a fire. In summer you might open the back door for a breath of cool air, but on dreary, wet days in any season and all through winter it was the best place to be.

*

Early, dark evenings during the war, without street lighting, and windows covered with blackout material, curtains tight drawn, winter seemed longer than ever and home more precious. Outside, the night would be thick enough to feel between your fingers, but in the kitchen, even without electric light, there was a glow to read by, if you were so inclined. Jac, tired, sleepy even, would gaze into the fire and read the stories there. He saw fighting figures, cities ablaze, volcanoes in the bubbling black pustules of coals venting gas in jets that spurted flame. It was cold beyond the fire's reach; better to change into warmed pyjamas there, run upstairs and dive beneath the weight of bedclothes to find the spot already hot-water-bottle-warmed between the sheets. That winter early in the conflict, when grey light announced another cold day, if you dared, you could look on panes feathered and forested by frost so thick a scraping finger dredged a layer of white under the nail.

But one lucky weekend the wind dropped and the low sun, though without heat, shone brightly enough to tempt Jimmy's gang to walk. All four wore scarves and gloves and stamped their feet to warm their toes. They crossed the bridge to the other side and, in close formation, tramped up the Rhiw towards the farms. The black path was flecked with flakes and harder than they could ever recall, the grass on either side stiff in frost-bearded tufts. Further on, gorse bushes were great shocks of grey and trees lining the top of the bank, bereft, struck attitudes of alarm and terror. At the top of the ridge, they passed the hay barn and walked on, warmer for the climb.

It was Eck who, glancing through a window in the thick thorn hedge, saw something, a big something, shining brilliantly on the slope beyond. 'What's that?' he said, and they all turned back to look.

Jimmy was uncertain, a rare condition for him.

'It's someone flashing a mirror,' Billy ventured.

'Don't be daft,' said Jimmy. 'Who'd have a mirror that big?'

'We could go and look,' said Eck. 'There's a gate just by there.'

The small gap through which they had been peering was too high for Jac to see the strange vision, but that was not unusual and he followed the others when they approached the gate. Jimmy set an example by climbing to the top bar, balancing a moment and leaping off. The effect was less spectacular than he had anticipated, because the landing ground, deep-rutted by the hooves of horses that came to the gate for food, or a change of view, had frozen into iron ridges. He limped aside, and his hortatory 'Forward!' had less verve than usual. Eck and Billy followed him by climbing up one side and down the other, while Jac, wary, squeezed himself between two lower bars.

Outside the sunken lane the landscape was more extensive. Two farmhouses were revealed, each in its sheltered hollow with grey smoke from chimneys rising straight into pale blue sky and windless air. Black scribbled hedges defined empty white fields. The view of the phenomenon also had changed. What had dazzled the vision shortly before was, from this fresh perspective, or in that lapse of time, different. It was now like a broad silver shield laid upon the breast of a low hill a few hundred yards off. After a moment's thought, Jimmy declared there were no horses or cattle to be wary of, for they were all indoors in the warm. There was nothing to stop them having a closer look.

The frosted grass they trod crunched beneath their feet, and it became clearer with each step that the white, glistening sheet drawn over the slope was ice. They reached a bank that had once marked a field-end topped by the straggling remains of a hedge interspersed with the trunks of taller trees, all winter bare and, at its foot, a rush- and moss-filled ditch. Above the bank, the ice extended twenty yards or more along the bottom of the slope and stretched up it fully thirty yards. It was magnificent. They gazed at it transfixed.

'Let's get to the top,' said Jimmy.

And they did, scrambling up the slippery tilt of the hill at the side of a broad river of ice, dully gleaming now as the declining sun had withdrawn its polish.

'How did it come here?' said Jac. 'We don't have ice like this our side.'

While Eck and Billy pondered the question, Jimmy said, 'I think it's because water is coming out of the hill – and usually it runs into that ditch at the bottom. That's why they dug the ditch. It's sort of seeping out all along here,' he added, pointing to the curious almost straight line of ice across the slope. 'And it's become frozen bit by bit, over and over again, until it stretches all the way to the old hedge at the bottom.'

It's lovely,' said Jac.

'How about a sledge-ride down?' Eck was enthused by the notion. 'You wouldn't 'alf go fast.'

'Whoosh!' said Billy. 'Whoosh! Like a rocket!'

'Is the ice very thick?' Jac gazed at it, fascinated.

'No – look,' said Jimmy, 'at the edge here – it's quite thin.' He dug at it with his heel and broke off a jagged fragment. 'See?'

Eck and Billy nodded. 'Yeh … quite thin really, I 'spect,' said Eck.

'But it's thicker by there.' Jac pointed vaguely to a spot a couple of feet into the layered ice.

'Well let's find out,' said Jimmy, stretching out his right leg and banging down with his heel.

What happened next left the others gaping and silent with shock, for the ice reached up and seized their leader.

'Aaaah!' he said, his voice wailing and tailing off as though it were written in a comic bubble.

He flew helplessly down the ice, first sitting, then on his back, arms flailing, legs in the air, before disappearing between two stout tree trunks and over the edge of the old field boundary.

'Jimmy!' Billy shouted after his brother's brief but heroic descent. 'Jimmy!'

All three ran and slithered down the frosted grassy slope to the top of the bank above the ditch, in which Jimmy lay dazed.

'You all right?' said Eck, while Billy stood dumb, on the verge of tears, and Jac came panting to view the victim.

'I think so.' Jimmy was stretched out on a bed of frost-decked rushes with every appearance of comfort. 'I seem to have made a soft landing.'

Then, pulling himself together, as they descended the bank to join him, 'That was a slide-and-a-half, wasn't it. You going to have a go?'

'Me? Not likely!' said Eck. 'You missed those trees by a whisker.'

'Bang! Wallop!' said Billy, recovering. 'Bang! Wallop! If you'd hit those trees.'

'Here – give us a hand,' said Jimmy.

They hoisted him to his feet and he brushed himself down.

'You've got all ice on your back,' said Jac, 'like a snowman.'

'It was great,' Jimmy said, but without conviction.

'The ice was thick, then. Quite thick?' said Jac.

'And quick!' said Eck and, without another thought about what might have happened, they all laughed.

*

Dada got Jo up early for work at the factory, because she had to be sure to catch the train. Apart from a chapel or club outing to the seaside, perhaps once a year in high summer, and often not even that, the valley had no passenger train service. Steam engines puffed up and down daily, but only to pull empty trucks to the sidings passing under the screens where they were loaded with coal, and down and away again. The war's hunger for munitions, and the need for more and more people to toil at making them, brought the valley's branch line into daily service for that purpose only. So Jo got up at six o'clock to have breakfast, which she ate mechanically, not tasting it, and ran the short distance to the station.

Standing, waiting on the unlit platform in winter darkness, there would already be a crowd of women, and a few older men, past soldiering, wearing Dai-caps. Some would be smoking, for once at the factory it was banned: a naked flame from match or lighter could precipitate catastrophe. It was always a subdued crowd. Few were any wider awake than Jo, and she moved and spoke by habit merely. The train would draw in, take them all on board, into compartments without lighting, and deposit them at another station. There, in darkness still, they would find buses waiting to take them to the factory, where Monday to Friday they worked from

7.30 am until 7.00 pm, when they emerged to make the return journey, again in blacked-out darkness. The Saturday shift was shorter, from 7.30 am to 1.00 pm. Sunday was, mercifully, still a day of rest.

For a long time Jo said nothing at home about her work. It was partly because she was too tired to talk and then the message daily drummed into them at the factory that 'Walls have ears', also had its effect. Eventually, as her mind and body became attuned to the new way of life, if pressed to say whether she was 'all right', and if then she was in the mood, she would say, 'Yes, I'm fine. I like it there. Really. We're all in it together. Everybody's friendly. We talk a lot – and we look out for one another – you know – "pull together".'

When summer came round and, going to and from work it was possible to see something of the site, she let slip that the factory was huge and she had only glimpsed a tiny part of it. Later still she said, 'I noticed soldiers this morning, as the bus was passing, standing outside this half-hidden concrete thing and I asked Beryl what it was – I usually sit on the bus with Beryl. We work in the same section, only she's been there a couple of years already – and she said, "It's a pillbox. There's machine guns in it to protect the factory. They've got them all around the place, manned day and night." And there were these two soldiers outside having a quiet cigarette.'

On another occasion, in the kitchen, a wet Sunday evening, Jac reading his comic, Mama knitting, Jo looking at the fire, musing, suddenly said, 'It's all camouflaged, of course, to hide it from the air. The roofs are grassed, so that they have, like, low tumps on top, and sheep on them. Sheep on them! Now who'd have thought they'd do something as strange as that? And there are huge, thick blast walls all over the place.'

Mama went on knitting, and Jac, who, with comic spread before his eyes, had been attentive to every word, said, 'They could have cows and a pond with ducks. I bet the Germans would think it's just an old farm and fly away. And good riddance!'

Jo smiled. 'Don't you say anything to anybody,' she said. 'Not a word.'

It was a 'filling factory'. There were more than thirty thousand working alongside her, packing explosives into bombs, shells, cartridges, mortar rounds, grenades – every kind of ammunition – for all the Forces, the army, the navy and the air force. It was very dangerous work. They all wore boiler suits, and turbans to cover their hair – because you were not allowed to have hairpins or clips of any kind. And no jewellery either.

'If I was married,' Jo said, 'and had a wedding ring that I couldn't take off, I would have to bind it up so nothing of it showed. They keep telling us – and they check every day – we mustn't bring anything into the factory that might start an explosion. One girl got into terrible trouble back in the winter when she brought a little torch in her bag to help her on her way home, because it's up a rough lane, where she lives I mean. At the start they said the torch could be used for signalling – that she was a spy.'

Tom, their father, loved both his children, would cheerfully have sacrificed himself for the sake of either, but there was a particularly strong bond between him and the first born, Jo, whom he had helped nurse through serious childhood illness and seen grow forthright and full of courage, with a natural affinity for horses resembling his own. Jo would tell her father about events, incidents, that she would never divulge to her mother, whose nature and indispositions made her anxious for everyone, and he would sit in the old armchair, head bowed, listening, his hair a silver halo in the firelight. So he knew there was one part of the factory where the women, and they were nearly all women, put slippers of asbestos over their shoes and could only shuffle along. It was dangerous, so horribly dangerous.

One evening, because the burden of it weighed heavily on her, Jo whispered to him, 'There was an accident today, just before dinner time. A box of detonators blew up and three were killed. We knew something had happened because we heard the bang – in the distance. It wasn't close to us. And then a whisper came to the shop about it. I couldn't eat a thing. No one could. They call them "the suicide squad" – the women who make the detonators – "the suicide squad".'

As on all these occasions, her father said nothing. He might nod or shake his head sadly. He felt a kind of terror, and a haunting sadness difficult to shake off, but what could he say?

Another time she said, 'Do you know what they call the explosive that's put in the big bombs? Those bombs – they weigh about half-a-ton! "Biscuit". I ask you, "biscuit", like Marie or cream crackers. They have a recipe, they say. They weigh TNT powder on scales. It's yellow stuff that gets onto your clothes, under your clothes, everywhere! They mix it with something called "nitrate", I think, and boil it all up and pour it onto trays to cool, then they break up this "biscuit" – sounds more like making toffee to me – and pack it into the bombs and pour more boiling TNT on top. How's that for tea Mr Hitler? The girls who do that have to drink some brown stuff which is supposed to keep their lungs clear.'

Contamination from the chemicals the women worked with

was inevitable and unavoidable. For a time, Jo worked with what they called 'gun cotton'. She didn't know much about it, except that it was dangerous, of course. She said, 'It looks just like cotton wool – but with a stink on it, such an awful chemically stink that sometimes a girl will pass out. I haven't passed out, not yet anyway, but it's all around me, seems to be inside me. It gets in your breath. It's horrible.'

Her mother's first appalled realisation and exclamation that Jo's face was going yellow brought a falsely gay reply, 'They call us "canaries". Yes, "canaries", that's what they say. Do you think a nice boy would go out with a canary?'

There was no further talk on the subject, even when her dark hair turned green.

The taint of the factory seeped everywhere. 'Where they're using TNT,' Jo told her father when they were alone, 'the walls have gone pink. I used to think pink was pretty – "Oh, I'd love a pink dress!" – now the thought of it turns me sick.'

The factory worked non-stop and shift work became the norm for all the women. There were weeks when Jo slept in the day and, even when on day shift, she was up and out so early and home so late and exhausted that Jac, with his own routine of early bedtimes at his mother's insistence, to be fresh and ready for school, saw her only occasionally and briefly.

She craved fresh air. 'I want to go somewhere I can breathe really deep breaths,' she often said and, on Sundays, even when the weather was foul, she would saddle Betsy, because she needed to ride as desperately as the horse needed exercise, and lead her up the cobbled path to the back of the terrace, close to the deserted church and the still gaping bomb crater and on to the mountain. She rode alone along the familiar paths and over the pathless further reaches of moorland above the valley tops, unfrequented even by sheep, where a breeze combing long grasses could freshen in a moment to a westerly gale, or mist and rain so erase the view that she would give Betsy her head, trusting the horse to pick her way safely home.

During one of these long rambles, on a pleasant summer day in the second year of the war, thinking of anything and nothing, lulled by the rhythm of the horse's steady plodding, she found herself in a lonely place of undulating humps and hollows skirting a patch of bog and seeing at some distance a tangle of wreckage. Even when she drew nearer it was difficult to discern a shape, but she knew it was the remains of an air crash. It was little more than crumpled framework, much of the plane having been removed as useful scrap, or by people hunting souvenirs, along with the dead airmen – unless they had bailed out. Closer still, she could see from what was left of camouflaged paintwork and a fragment of insignia that it had been an enemy plane. It was probably a bomber, she thought, because some months earlier there had been raids night after night on Liverpool and other towns and cities with terrible destruction and loss of life. She wondered what had brought it down.

She leaned forward in the saddle and spoke to Betsy and to herself quietly: 'Could have been the pilot, in black night, simply flew into the mountain. Or perhaps it hit an air pocket. They say other planes, ours, have come down due to air pockets over the mountains.'

'I hope it was brought down by shells or bullets,' she said and the horse, well used to these one-sided conversations, nodded its head, as though it understood. 'I hope it was brought down by shells and bullets I helped to make!'

Then she thought of the terror of the air crew when a plane

is hit, knowing it is going down, and the misery of parents, wives and children when it fails to return, and she felt a burning hatred for the maniac Hitler and his mad gang. She leaned forward again and patted the neck of the chestnut with a feeling of great tenderness.

'I think I prefer animals to people,' she said, and then, laughing, ' – even Dinah.'

Obedient to her gentle twitch of the rein the horse turned and, knowing it was heading for home, at the same steady pace retraced its steps.

*

Having conducted a lone reconnaissance mission there, Jimmy led his platoon to the river bank in the next stage of their manoeuvres. The stream ran clear down a steep slope at the top end of the valley until it reached the first of several colliery spoil heaps down which poured load upon load of slag and dust. Day after day, long trains of drams, each full to overflowing, were hauled to the top of the tip where crane-like gear upended them one at a time and sent their contents crashing and tumbling down almost to the water's edge. Over years of tipping, the slag had built into a mountain range, black, devoid of vegetation, and the stream had been deep-dyed the same dead colour. Except that it wasn't quite dead. A few water creatures persisted: small, polished black eels and fish known locally as 'scrachans' that were sluggishly brown and had feelers on their faces to help them find their way around in the darkness. How these survived, what they fed on, other than coal dust, was a mystery.

The narrow strip of river bank that remained was littered

with large blocks of shale that chance had so turned they bowled end over end down the tip, attaining sufficient momentum to reach the bottom, where they became obstacles for the gang to leap or avoid, or use as cover from an ever watchful and ruthless enemy. The troop followed Jimmy as he jumped and dodged, then dived and remained still until his raised arm motioned them forward again. At last, without losses, they broke clear of the encroaching waste from the two collieries at the upper end of the valley. It had been exhilarating and all had gone well, but now, as they rounded a bend in the stream, Jimmy's objective came into view and his carefully reconnoitred plan became clear.

Ahead was the barrier of the tall, steep-sided embankment that carried the road connecting one side of the valley to the other. This high causeway was itself a tip. Though more purposeful and shapely than the others, it was constructed from the same materials, the slag waste separated from untold thousands of tons of coal brought up from underground mixed with ashes from the engine houses that produced the steam to drive colliery machinery. The road that children trod daily to and from school, and along which Bonny had bolted, was a straight, flat strip laid on top, asphalt studded with gravel. Jimmy's gang, gathered on the river bank at its foot, looked up at this fresh challenge.

'What do we do? Climb up there, over the railings at the top and then cross the road, over the next lot of railings and down the other side?' Eck's question was in all minds.

Jimmy shook his head, and looked at Billy and Jac. 'What do you think?'

'That seems the best way to me,' Billy said, while Jac shrugged helplessly.

'If you do that, the enemy will have you in his sights every step of the way. He'll pick you off – no trouble at all. You've 'ad it!'

'All right then – you tell us how to do it.'

Jimmy pointed to the base of the embankment, where the black stream disappeared into a hole. 'There,' he said, with a note of triumph, 'through the culvert.'

Eck laughed. 'We're going swimming. Right under Jerry's nose. Fat chance!'

'Freddy told me how to do it. And I've done it, by myself.' Jimmy spoke quietly. 'I've done it – and I'll show you how.'

In a hundred yards or so they had reached the perfectly circular entrance of a brick-lined tunnel, about six feet in diameter, which channelled the stream under the embankment. They all peered through it to the small circle of light the other end, about fifty yards off. It was summer, the water low. Marks, pale green and yellow streaked with black, far higher on the brick walls either side of the water, showed the level it reached in spate.

'You can't mean we're supposed to wade through?' said Eck. 'I had a row for getting my shoes soaked. Though I suppose we could take them off and carry them.'

'I mustn't do that,' Jac said.

'Don't worry – we're going to climb along the side like flies.' Billy was scornful.

'I told you I've done it. And without getting wet at all.'

'Go on then. Show us.'

Steadying himself at the brick entrance, Jimmy stepped onto the curve of the culvert with his right foot just above the level of the water and immediately thrust himself off diagonally to the other side of the runnel, then thrust off the left to land clear of the water on the right once more, and so on, without pause, because to stop would have jeopardised his balance; he continued, a curiously fluttering, zig-zagging, gradually diminishing silhouette against the distant circle of light, until at the far end he leapt out of sight.

'He's gone,' said Jac.

'He's gone an' done it!' said Eck.

A moment later Jimmy's head appeared, a black dot at the remote edge of the brick tube, and his voice came hollowly echoing along it. 'I'm not a bit wet. All you got to do is keep going. It's easy. Come on.'

Eck looked at Billy and Jac. 'What do you think? It looks OK. Who's next?'

'Not me,' said Billy. 'You have a go.'

'It's this or all the way up to the top and over. Well, look out shoes: might as well try.'

He gingerly stepped into the culvert, holding on to the brick edge as long as he dared before, to save himself from toppling or sliding into the water, he jumped. What began as a stuttering and uncertain progress gradually acquired fluency as he copied Jimmy's zig-zag technique and it was with a shout of triumph that the final jump removed him from view.

Two black dots appeared at the rim of the circle of light and two voices chorused, 'Come on, come on! It's great! You can do it!'

'Ah well,' said Billy, 'we'd better try – or we'll be court-marshalled for cowardice. If Eck can do it …'

After steadying himself at the entrance, he thrust off in the way the brave, pioneering tunnel-runners had demonstrated and quite quickly fell into the same side-to-side rhythm, which brought him dry-shod to the distant exit.

'Come on, Jac. Your turn,' he shouted back.

Having seen Billy, too, successfully complete the run, for run it was – a leaping run in which the runner dared not pause or all was lost – Jac ventured his right foot on the slimed bricks at the entrance and, taking a deep breath, with a long jump-stride, reached the other side of the stream with his left. He hadn't fully appreciated that, having gone thus far, it was no longer possible to stop or turn back. He kept going, not daring to lift his eyes beyond the yard of brick-lined tube ahead and his feet landing ever closer to the stream.

A chorus of voices, gradually increasing in volume, encouraged him: 'Come on Jac!'; 'You can do it!'; 'Only a bit more!' But his friends had succeeded because they possessed the advantage of longer legs and his were tiring before he'd reached halfway. Above the sound of his own shortened breath he heard the splashes signalling the end of the culvert, and then his right foot landed in the water and slipped on the submerged bricks, so that he sat down suddenly and slid, and the stream carried him, still sitting, out into the open and he sank to his shoulders in the gouged exit pool.

Eager hands grabbed and dragged him out. 'That was great Jac! You did it!'

Breathless and shaking with shock and the chill of near total immersion, he could only whimper. When he was able to draw breath it was to howl, 'I want to go home,' and a moment later, 'I can't go home like this. O Mama, I can't go home like this.'

Arms out from his sides, water dripping from the tips of his fingers, running down his legs, oozing from his clothes, he seemed on the point of melting, dissolving into the stream that, released from the dark, was carrying on cheerfully enough considering the burden of coal dust it carried. The faces of his friends displayed a mixture of concern, fascination and barely suppressed hilarity, until Jimmy took charge of the situation.

'We're going to make you leader of amphibious operations,' he said, which stopped Jac's sobbing, because he was uncertain what it meant. 'We'll go to our house,' Jimmy went on. 'Our Ma will help. We'd better run to warm you up. Can you run? Did you swallow any water? I don't think it's good for you – though the scrachans manage.'

Confused by his ducking and Jimmy's words, Jac's lower lip quivered again.

'Squad at the double,' said Jimmy, grabbing his wet hand and setting off at a trot. 'Forward!'

Jac allowed himself to be hauled into motion and was soon trotting alongside the others to the bridge over the stream, where they scrambled up the bank and on to the path the colliers used on their way to and from work, and so, over the boarded railway lines at the station and up the road. There, breathless, his progress slowed to a squelching trudge, leaving a damp trail all along the pavement to Jimmy and Billy's.

He was tutted over by their mother, who, long accustomed to her boys' minor calamities, stripped the wet things off him and wrapped him in a blanket, stuffed pages of yesterday's newspaper in his shoes and set them on the fender where they steamed before the fire, and ran his clothes through the mangle to squeeze as much water as she could out of them before ironing them hissingly. A little later, they were not dry, but at first sight certainly not as wet as they had been. Jac, silent and quite snug in his blanket, was reluctant to put the damp things on and shivered at their clammy contact with his skin. But he was better again when Mrs Evans gave him a cup of warm milk and a biscuit. 'Tell your mother you had an accident – fell in the water – which is the truth – and I said you really should have a bath. It will be all right, you'll see.'

He did just that, without a word about running the culvert. His mother said, 'I don't think you should go out with those boys again. Make friends with someone your own age.'

Jac said, 'Can I have a cup of warm milk, please? Are there any biscuits?'

\*

The winter of the third year of war was as harsh as the two that preceded it. On a Sunday morning in the middle of January, Jac lay awake, aware that breakfast was ready, for a familiar aroma had risen through the house. Bacon was frying. It came from the much diminished portion of well-salted pig, hanging from the hook in the kitchen ceiling, which at this stage had only the meagrest streak of brownish lean meat. But the copious melted fat had a heady perfume irresistible to the hungry.

It was still outside, as though nature and life itself were muffled, and a strange, pale light penetrated the weave of the curtains of his room. He was warm beneath the blankets but his exposed nose, which had detected the appetising fragrance of breakfast, was cold. He knew that stepping out of bed onto icy lino would be a shock, as would taking off pyjamas and putting on clothes. Steeling himself to face the challenge, he leapt out and dressed as quickly as he could. Opened curtains revealed another day's harvest of stark white frost flowers spread across the window panes and, at the clearer edges, glimpses of a world where the multitudinous colours of daily life in the valley had been replaced by a uniform dead pallor.

'Snow!' he said, and hurried downstairs.

In her chair in the corner by the fire, his mother was sipping tea, holding the cup in both hands for the glow of warmth it brought.

'It's typical,' she said. 'Jo had to go into work today. She told us there's a big push on – and now this weather! We were just wondering whether she caught her train – or if there was a train. There must have been: she hasn't come back. It will be a struggle to get anywhere today for a lot of people.'

The fire was a great glowing mass of coals, red and yellow, and the kettle hummed a cheerful morning tune on the polished hob. It was lovely in the kitchen and never better than on a morning of frost and snow.

'Can I have fried bread and jam?' Jac said.

His mother patted damp a thick slice of yesterday's bread with water from the tap and placed it hissing in the hot melted bacon fat in the frying pan on the fire.

'I'll need to clear the yard,' his father said, 'or it's going to be a nuisance getting coal for the fires. It's been drifting. You can help if you want, after breakfast. And I've still got to see to Betsy.'

The bread from the pan was crisp brown outside, melting white inside. His mother spread blackberry jam and cut it into finger slices, and made him a cup of milky tea.

Beneath the table, Dinah, roused by the renewed scent of bacon fat and instantly aware someone was eating, struggled to her feet, her bulk grinding a chair back in the process. A black head emerged, long ears dangling like a luxuriantly bewigged hanging judge. Her brown eyes fixed on Jac as he ate, every motion of his hand, every morsel he put to his lips.

He knew the dog was there waiting, as always, and dropped a fragment of crust. Before it reached the floor, her jaws parted revealing rows of gleaming teeth and snapped it up. For all her ungainliness, she was capable of remarkable feats of speed, especially where food was concerned, or the slightest sound that might signal the approach of an intruder on her territory.

Dada opened the door and, as though it had been waiting for the opportunity, a chill blast brusquely entered.

'Oh, shut the door Tom,' Mama said, crouching nearer the fire.

In the moment before it closed, Jac saw how snow had gathered on the threshold in an exquisite windswept curve extending almost halfway up one side of the doorpost. 'It looks beautiful,' he said, though his immediate instinct was to knock it down.

'H'm, looks is one thing,' his mother said. 'If you do go out, put your wellies on and wrap-up warm.'

By the time he had dressed for the outdoors to his mother's satisfaction with jumper, scarf and gloves, and one of Jo's tams, which he resisted, pulled down over his ears, Dada had demolished the snow wave on the doorstep, cleared a path to the coalhouse and brought in a bucket of coal to feed the fire through the morning.

'I'd better take a shovel up the stable,' he said. 'Do you want to come and help?'

In the garden, everything was fresh transformed: corrugations of the coalhouse roof planed to a smooth canopy; frost-hard, turned garden soil corrugated white; stone walls on either side topped with sugar icing; bare branches and twigs of lilac bright, fine lines underscored with black. Where it had not billowed against or over an obstruction, the snow was almost to the top of Jac's wellingtons. He set out with a feeling of elation, making first marks in pristine whiteness up the path, but by the time he reached the back gate, lifting high his rubber-shod feet at each step, he was ready to follow, as best he could, in his father's footsteps, like the page in the Christmas carol.

Outside, the ash path had disappeared and the mountain beyond was a monstrous white wall of indeterminate height merging with the grey of the sky. Footprints here and there along the back road and a few half-cleared patches told where early risers had been busy, but at this time no one else was about. Steep steps down to the pavement from most of the terraced houses had yet to be cleared and spread with salt. No sign of life or light was visible in their black, frost-smeared front-windows, for families were gathered round their big kitchen fires at the back. It all seemed suddenly somewhere else, a strange, muffled world, the colliery, the railway line still, as though waiting for a sign. In the silence, which seemed to forbid talk, Jac heard the sound of his breathing, the crunch of his and his father's footsteps. If it had not been so cold, through his layers of clothing, the tam and gloves, he might have thought he was dreaming, to the plodding of their feet and with the slipperiness of dreams.

Just at the end of the terrace, they were both startled when a heap of snow piled against the outside wall of the last house erupted and two sheep sheltering beneath the drift leapt in fright at their near approach and then stood wrapped in dirty, snow-draggled fleeces looking at them with baleful amber eyes.

'Well, that wakes you up,' Jac's father said. 'Come on. Not

far now.' And in another few minutes they were carefully stepping over the slippery cobbles of the familiar lane leading down to the stable.

As they opened the door of the yard, his father pushing hard against snow, Jac heard the horse whinny.

'She's calling to us,' he said.

'She's wanting her breakfast.'

His father was already briskly shovelling a narrow path to the stable door. 'Yes, she's hungry, just like you were. And I'm sure she'll be glad of a bit of company for a while. Horses get lonely. You like being with your friends, don't you? Well, horses do, too. Jo can't get up here as often as she'd wish and, since Bonny's gone, Betsy's been on her own. It's a pity really. She hasn't anyone to pass the time of day with. I've known horses that have made friends with a dog, and won't go anywhere unless the dog goes too.'

Betsy's stall possessed an animal warmth after the cold outdoors. With the light on, the pony glowed chestnut and she snuffled and nodded her head to show she was glad to see them.

'Perhaps I could be her friend,' said Jac. 'I could sleep in the stable with her and talk to her a bit. If Mama would let me have a blanket, I could wrap up in it and sleep in the straw.' He became excited elaborating the idea. 'And we could talk until she was sleepy.'

'I'm sure she'd like that – but your mother wouldn't. We'll just come up now and again and make sure she's got plenty to eat and drink.' He busied himself with sacks of chaff and oats and refilling the water bucket. 'You could help now by sweeping out and getting fresh straw. That will warm you up a bit before we start back.'

Accustomed to this part of the routine, Jac brushed vigorously around and under the horse until the floor was clear, from time to time patting the horse's neck and saying a few friendly words to her.

'Don't worry about brushing out into the yard,' his father said. 'That will have to wait until I've cleared the snow outside. It won't hurt for a day or so in the empty stall.'

Together they spread fresh straw and, having checked everything was in order, listened for a moment to Betsy munching contentedly before switching off the light and opening the door to the cold. The walk up the slippery narrow way between hotel and stable-yard wall did not prepare them for the change in the weather that struck them as they emerged from its shelter. They turned to face a keen wind with blown lying snow and fresh flurries on its icy breath.

'Come on, the sooner we get back the better,' his father said, bowing his head into the stinging gusts.

Although barely eleven o'clock, the day was already darkening. The terraced houses, without a sign of light or life, for families were still gathered round kitchen fires, stared blankly down on a wasteland and two hunched figures. Jac thought to use the path they had made through the snow on the way up to the stable, but it was filling and disappearing before his eyes and he was soon floundering. He made better progress using his father as a windbreak and taking long strides to match the fresh footprints. Although thus sheltered a little from the buffeting of the wind, the warmth he had gained from helping in the stable soon ebbed away and he began to tire and fall behind and feel very cold. His father turned and saw he was struggling.

'It's not far now,' he said. 'Nearly home. Come here, good

boy. Hold round my neck.' And he lifted Jac and carried him cwtched in his arms along the backs of their neighbours' houses, to their own grumbling back gate, safely down the snowbound garden path, past the gaping coalhouse doorway, through the back door and into the kitchen.

Jac was crying a little from the pain of the cold and the shame of being carried like a baby.

'There you are at last,' Mama said. 'Take those things off and come and sit by the fire. The kettle's just boiled. I'll make us all a nice cup of tea, and you can tell me how Betsy's getting on. Let's get these wellies off. My goodness your feet are soaking. No wonder they're cold.'

'I'm cold all over,' Jac said. 'My fingers and toes are stinging.'

'But it was nice outside, I expect. Like explorers in the Arctic.'

'No, it was horrible,' Jac said, adding, with vehemence, 'I hate snow.'

*

It was not a great surprise when the electricity failed later that afternoon, because it had happened before. 'Icing on the power lines again, I expect,' said Jac's father, rummaging in a drawer for candles. He heated the candle ends over the fire till they dripped and lodged them securely in the two larger brass candlesticks on the mantelpiece.

Jac put aside the comic he was reading, his father folded the newspaper and his mother placed the embroidery she was working on and the skeins of coloured silk thread in her basket. Jac liked the light of the flickering candles and the fire in the kitchen. Though not enough to read by, it brought them all closer together within the warmth of family. His mother and his father felt it, too.

After a while of silent contemplation, 'I hope this weather won't stop Jo's train,' Mama said.

'It will be all right – it's very cold, but there hasn't been much fresh snow since this morning and it ran then.'

'Well, I've got her dinner in the oven.'

'Can we have the wireless on?' said Jac.

Listening to the wireless was a perfect way of passing the time, especially in ruddy, fitful light when imagination was freed to conjure pictures. *ITMA* was Jac's favourite. He greeted the programme's many catch-phrases like old friends: 'It's bein' so cheerful as keeps me goin'', 'Dis is Funf speaking', 'Don't forget the diver, sir', 'Ta-ta for now'. Everybody knew them, as they knew the meaning of the dot-dot-dot-dash drumbeat that filled spaces between programmes, and as they knew the voice of the man they called 'Lord Haw-Haw' saying 'Jarmany calling, Jarmany calling', threatening, cajoling, with an edge of menace.

Along with 'Music While You Work' and the comedians with their jokes on 'Workers' Playtime' and other entertainments, there was also, always, the news, news of the war. In that third winter of fighting, the evening's news of battles, raids, enemy aircraft destroyed, mentioned the arrival of American soldiers in Britain, because the Japanese attack on Pearl Harbour and invasion of the Philippines had brought the USA into the war. And it told how the terrible Russian winter added to the suffering of the people of Leningrad, already months under siege and seemingly at the mercy of German forces determined to kill everyone and obliterate the city.

'Oh, the poor people,' Mama murmured, 'the poor people.'

'Will they have snow there?' Jac, too, was listening and wondering.

'Yes, much, much worse than our bit of snow,' his father said. 'You would never believe how cold it is there. Their winter goes on and on, cold enough to freeze your fingers and toes right off. And I don't think the people come home to fires like this one we have, or nice hot dinners.'

Jac was quiet and thoughtful, but it was difficult to imagine the pain of others.

'Children just your age are suffering there – in all that cold, with the bombs and shells coming down and destroying their homes. You ought to pray for them,' Mama said. 'Pray for all the poor, poor people.'

Jac was silent, but for a moment his eyes glistened in the firelight.

*

Jac did not heed his mother's encouragement to find new friends. It was partly a question of convenience and proximity. He had other friends, boys in his own class at school, but almost all of them lived in streets some small distance off and were in their own local gangs. The few who lived nearby were not nearly so interesting as Jimmy and Billy and Eck. With Jimmy, you never quite knew where you would go, or what would happen when you got there. He had learned a great deal from following in the adventurous footsteps of his older brother, and having got into a lot of uncomfortable scrapes with Freddy, he had no qualms about inflicting similar risks on his younger brother and anyone else who happened along.

And then there was constant news of the war to inspire him. It was no wonder Jac's mother was on pins whenever she watched him, usually at the tail end of the little gang as it wound its way out of sight up the mountain. However difficult it was to keep up, Jac followed.

Jimmy had been keen on science ever since receiving a junior chemistry set for Christmas a few years before. He had grown a crystal in one experiment and made an awful stink with another, but the range of materials and possible uses was limited and his interest waned. A teacher in the Big School revived his enthusiasm by showing the class that scientists were people who had enquiring minds and set themselves to solve problems by experimenting over and over again. For Jimmy, this chimed with his readiness to try new routes and destinations, new ways of doing things, and to ask himself the question 'What if …' when most others would have sensibly decided not to bother.

Along with the collection of comics, he inherited from Freddy a box containing odd bits of Meccano that had little potential and were soon put aside, and a hand-cranked generator from which dangled two leads to which small metal cylinders of a size to fit in the palm of a hand were attached. The one purpose of the machine was to demonstrate how, by vigorously turning the handle, you could produce an electric current. However, if you turned the handle, you could not, at the same time, feel the electricity: for demonstration purposes the scientist had to have at least one assistant. Naturally, Jimmy called on his brother.

Billy had grown wary over the years and, from time to time, would resist invitations, requests and even commands – and then there would be a row. But knowing electricity came out of plugs and sockets, when you put a switch on, and doubtful of the potential of an inert metal cylinder contraption to do anything very much, on this occasion he agreed to participate in the experiment.

Just then Jac knocked at the front door. 'They're round the back,' Mrs Evans said. 'They've found some old thing of Freddy's. Go and see what they're up to.'

He arrived just as Billy was taking up the terminals at the end of the leads. 'What you doing?' he asked.

'Making electricity.'

'How?'

'By turning this handle as fast as you can. I'll show you.' Jimmy wound away at the handle, watching for any reaction.

It did not take long for Billy to throw the terminals aside with a yell. 'I had a shock,' he said, jumping about and shaking his hands vigorously, '– a 'lectric shock. I'm not doing that again.'

'What was it like? Did it hurt?'

'Well, it was a tingle,' he said, 'Went from my hand right up my arm.'

'Have you got a cut? Did it burn?' Jac, too, was curious.

'Let's see,' said Jimmy grasping one of Billy's hands. 'Look – not a mark. Nothing. It didn't hurt at all really – did it?'

'Go on then, you hold those things and I'll wind the handle.'

'All right. Carry on!' Jimmy picked up the terminals. 'Look – I'm holding them tight. Now you turn it.'

Billy gripped the handle with a smile and wound away furiously. Jimmy's eyes opened wide, his cheeks turned pink, then he danced up and down on his toes, before laying the terminals down neatly but hurriedly.

'Yes … it does … give you … quite a smart tingle,' he said, assuming cool self-control. 'Makes you want to jump about a bit. I think if you hold only one of the terminals it doesn't work. There's got to be a circuit. One in each hand and the circuit's complete.'

Jac looked at him. This was all new knowledge, and interesting. 'I'll hold one terminal,' he said, 'to experiment, while you turn the handle.'

'OK,' said Jimmy. 'Billy, you do the winding.'

Jac picked up one of the metal cylinders, held it in his hand and, not entirely trusting Jimmy's hypothesis, closed his eyes, hoping for the best. Nothing happened. He opened his eyes. 'Did you wind it?'

'Yes,' said Billy, 'I wound like the devil!'

'Hold both the terminals,' said Jimmy, 'and see how that feels.'

'No – you've done that experiment already,' said Jac, after a moment's thought.

Jimmy shrugged. 'Right. I've got an idea. Jac, what if you hold one terminal and Billy, you hold the other? Will that make a circuit?'

They tried it, each holding a cylinder, first in one hand, then the other, while Jimmy wound away. Nothing happened. No tingle, nothing.

'Oh – I know, I know!' said Jimmy, with a note of triumph. 'Both of you hold a cylinder with one hand and, Billy, you hold Jac's hand with the other. Right, that's it. Now then: I'm going to wind the handle like billy-o, so you can look out.'

'Like Billy did?'

'Ah, yes – but no. I'm going to wind it very fast: like billy-o.'

Then, seeing Jac was still confused, 'Never mind, you just hold that thing tight.'

And he wound the handle like billy-o – and the electricity surged from the machine along the lead, through the little cylinder in one hand up the arm and down the other arm, and into the clasped hand and up the next arm and down the other to the hand grasping the second little cylinder, and down the other lead back to the machine, round and round, tingling Jac and Billy until they danced and shouted and dropped the little cylinders.

'It works! It works!' said Jimmy. 'I told you – it works!'

\*

Day after school day, year after year, Jac walked to morning lessons, home for dinner, back again in the afternoon and home for tea. Closing the clinking gate carefully behind him to stop marauding sheep getting into the front garden, he walked by the Italian corner shop where, before the war, you could buy ice-cream, and sweets without coupons, round the corner, past the Workmen's Hall with its cinema and library and billiard tables, over the steel-girdered bridge above the railway lines, along the tarmac strip that Bonny had galloped, up a straight hill between rows of terraced houses, over a brook, to the open space where, long before, the schools had been sited either side of a liberally potholed, unmade extension of that brief side street off the road around the valley.

Summer holidays over, at the beginning of the third year of the war, he found himself going to a different school building, because the Boys' Elementary stood on a bank opposite the Infants' and the Girls' school on their shared site. All three looked the same, were made of the same materials, dirty grey stone trimmed at doors and windows with red brick, had the same tall, many-paned windows set so high in recesses in the walls not even the tallest pupil could see through them to life outside, stout doors, slated roofs and sloping asphalt yards for playtime, and were surrounded by the same tall spiked railings, whether to impound the young within or keep their elders out was not declared. Now, what there was of daylight entering all the classrooms was filtered through broad, crossed strips of brown paper pasted to every pane, lest bomb blast should shatter them to maiming, killing splinters.

In the 'Big School' Jac seemed suddenly to see more clearly, like some pup or kitten with freshly opened eyes, the setting and circumstances into which time, his age, had delivered him. The boys, well-scrubbed and grubby, tidy and ragged, sat in pairs in rows of double desks with cast iron frames, stout hinged seats and slopes of heavy wood decorated with an inset white ceramic inkwell either side. All desks bore gouged symbols of passing generations, ingrained stains of spilled ink, and once seated even small boys like him found movement in or out, up or down, restricted: it was rather like confinement in an up-dated model of the stocks. This was not the only difference from the Infants'. The helpful pictorial reminders of the alphabet – A for apple, B for ball … S for snake … Z for zebra – no longer decked the walls. No pictures of any kind hung above the dado of glossy institutional tiles. On early darkening days as autumn came, bare light bulbs sometimes flared under pearly shades like Chinese coolie hats and the hefty silver concertinas of cast iron radiators hummed with heat. That very first term the fireplace in the corner remained unlit and its bucket of coal was mantled with chalk-dust, but in other winters through the war it blazed and smoked gustily most days and from time to time the morning crate of milk, tabs on icy stalks, stood in the hearth.

There were blackboards, one on an easel and one in a frame set into the wall beside the teacher's heavy desk, throne-like, on massive wooden runners, from which he surveyed the room to the distant corners. The only embellishment of any kind, hung by its crook from a top corner of the blackboard, was a slim, whippy cane. In Jac's first year it was rarely unhooked and brandished with intent, but times and teachers changed. A new headmaster, hair, jowls and suit a grey man, announced a no-nonsense regime. He emerged from his own cigarette-smoke filled room at the appointed hour morning and afternoon to open the school door and ring a brass handbell vigorously, at which the pupils assembled on the yard in class lines and trooped in. When the last had passed by him, he closed the door and remained standing on the step outside, tawse in hand, to greet each latecomer in turn with a stinging slap on the palm.

Few remained entirely unacquainted with tawse and cane, while some, unpunctual, more talkative, less diligent, impertinent even, boldly careless of consequences, met them frequently, and these encounters punctuated days otherwise predictably routine: arithmetic exercises, English exercises, reading aloud round the class. At playtime, while happily enough sucked into the maelstrom of the yard, Jac warily avoided collision with the big boys of upper standards chafing for release to the pit, each accompanied by a small shoal of hangers-on, lest they unaccountably and without rancour inflicted a knuckly punch to back or biceps or a Chinese burn. Occasional afternoon curricular variations were greeted with unfeigned delight, whether it was to join with another class for singing ('To be a pilgrim' ,'Molly Malone', 'Some talk of Alexander'), or copying with a pencil a scene of cliff and sea and bent, breeze-blasted tree chalk-sketched by the teacher on the blackboard, or at wide intervals listening to him reading the beginning of a story from a stout book. That it was always the same story and the same few pages mattered not at all.

*

About this time, it began to be apparent all was not well with the straight road to the other side. Those whose eyes were not constantly fixed on the hills ahead and the sky above, noticed blemishes in the tarmac, and then narrow fissures, as though the road's skin was diseased. Gradually, so that you would not see changes from day to day, or even week to week, the cracks grew more numerous and widened. At last, even the chronically unobservant could not help suspecting that something insidious and malign was at work, because on wet days, which were not uncommon, wisps of smoke rose here and there from the crazed surface, as though it rained warm drops straight from some cloud-hidden kettle. More tellingly, when there was little or no wind to pull the wisps away, and they climbed knee high and higher, the awful smell of them rose about you. It was like being in a whole roomful of Jimmy's stink bombs.

After one particularly damp and malodorous walk home, Jac asked his mother about the awful smell coming from the road.

'I'm not sure I know,' she said. 'It will be something to do with the colliery, I expect. You'd better ask your father.'

He did, and his father, who knew about the creasing and cracking of the macadamised surface and the horrid smell that rose from it in wet weather, told Jac how the road had been built on top of a great pile of slag and other colliery waste and the river channelled underneath the heap.

'I've seen the culvert,' said Jac. 'Jimmy showed us.'

'It can be dangerous,' his father said, 'especially in winter after heavy rain, when the water almost fills it. You keep away from it. Keep away from that filthy river altogether.'

'Yes, Dada.'

He was quiet for a while, thinking, with a certain pride, that he had run the brick-lined tunnel, though he was the youngest and the smallest of Jimmy's gang, almost to the end, and if he hadn't slipped, it would have been a triumph. 'I'm bigger now,' he thought, '– a bit. I 'spect I could do it now without getting wet.' He was tempted to show off about it to his father. Mama had probably told him about the soaking in the river, but how it came about was still a secret between him, the gang and Mrs Evans.

He decided not to. 'But why does it stink up on the road?' he said.

'They weren't careful what they put on the tip. They just wanted to make as big a pile as they could as quickly as possible to build the road on top. When I was young there wasn't a road to the other side and no buses or cars could go round the valley. There were only paths like those on the mountain. Because they were in a hurry, they used ash and coke from the colliery boilers as well as the slag, and some loads were still glowing hot like those lumps of coal in the fire. Then they piled more slag and waste on top – on and on – thinking it would all die down safe enough. But it didn't.

It's been smouldering quietly for decades now. Not big flames, just quiet smouldering away and there's smoke coming off it all the time, but you see it – and smell it – mostly when it's wet. You'd get the same sort of smoke and stench if you emptied a cupful of water on the fire in the grate. But we're not going to try that. You'll just have to take my word for it.'

★

One Saturday morning, after the cinema matinée show in which Flash Gordon had thwarted the evil designs of the Emperor Ming again, but ended up in grave danger from Ming's helmeted men and a ray-gun, Jac met Jimmy and Billy on their way home from scavenging on the ash-tip. Jimmy was carrying their latest find, a petrol can. Or was it for something else, water even? He shook it, but there was no sound of liquid chuckling inside.

'Whatever's there, it isn't much,' he said.

'Why don't you open it?' said Jac.

'What a brilliant idea!' said Billy with a scornful look. 'The cap's stuck, so we're going to take it down our garden to see if we can find out.'

Jac, with time to spare before dinner, joined them. As there had been a few days without rain, they sat on the dry grass where the tent was sometimes pitched and examined the can. It was patched with rust and a little dented, but at first glance appeared sound.

'What you going to do with it?' Jac was curious.

'Don't know yet. First job – get this cap off,' Jimmy said and he disappeared indoors. With nothing to do and not much to say, Jac and Billy looked down the garden and beyond to the black incline, where a line of empty drams, spragged and stationary, waited for the next shift, and the screens were silent. There were few hours in the week when the colliery, or at least that part of it on the surface, was mostly quiet. Turnover between shifts sometimes brought such momentary relief from the clangour and racket of everyday work, when birds seemed suddenly to be shouting their joy to be alive.

Preceded by Dash, wafting his fan-like tail and eagerly sniffing at everyone and everything, Jimmy returned with pliers, a screwdriver and an oil squirt can, small and round with a tapering snout, that his mother used to lubricate her sewing machine.

'Mam won't mind,' he said, oiling the stubborn cap liberally, before attacking it from various angles with the pliers and the screwdriver. Billy was smiling broadly at his brother's frustration when whatever clenching of the screw, or crust of rust, yielded and, voicing a small grinding squeak, the cap turned. With a triumphant 'There you are!' he unscrewed it.

'Now what?' said Billy.

Jimmy looked thoughtful. First, he shook the can again. It was silent as before. Then he turned it upside down. No liquid emerged. He sniffed it. 'I think it's had petrol in.'

'Why did they throw it away?' Jac was intrigued by the wastefulness of the former owner.

'It's only a bit dented.'

'H'm,' said Jimmy, examining the can carefully. 'I think that could be the reason.' He pointed to a seam low on one side of the can where a small, dark stain suggested a leak. 'Even with a tiny leak, they wouldn't want to keep petrol in it, if they ever did. We can find that out.' And he disappeared into the kitchen again, returning almost at once with a box of matches.

'Experiment number one,' he said, and, while Billy and Jac watched carefully, he bent towards the can and lit a match. A passing breeze blew it out. He lit a second match and, shielding the timid flame with his other hand, leaned closer to drop it into the open neck.

With an instantaneous loud thump the can leapt into the air. Jimmy leapt in another direction, Dash set off for the house, tail between his legs, and Billy and Jac threw themselves to the ground. When they struggled upright again, they saw the can lay a couple of yards off in a row of leeks, where Dash, with fresh courage, returned to crouch and bark at it. Jimmy looked dazed and subtly altered by the experiment. The hair on his forehead was shorter and his ginger eyebrows had been erased. Jac was speechless with shock, as was Billy for just a moment, before he began to laugh.

'That was an experiment-and-a-half,' he said and, looking at Jimmy, laughed again. 'The best ever!'

*

In the autumn of 1942, newsreels had shown the allied artillery barrage at the beginning of the battle of El Alamein in the Egyptian desert, flashes in black night from a line of field guns extending for miles and going on for hours. But that was only the beginning. It was early summer of 1943 before the desert victory was assured. Cinema audiences saw fresh pictures of shabby columns of German and Italian soldiers, with drooping shoulders and glum, exhausted expressions, shuffling to captivity under the guns of a handful of grim-faced Allied troops. What remained of the enemy in North Africa had surrendered.

There were occasional air raids still, but not over the valley and the voice of the siren was rarely heard. The threat of invasion had died away. Nevertheless, the Home Guard continued practising at a firing range on open ground beyond the schools on the other side. Empty brass cartridge cases, overlooked in long grass when sessions ended, but spotted later by keener-eyed searchers, were occasionally traded during playtime for stamps or marbles.

It had been unusually dry, and with longer evenings as well as weekends at their disposal, Jimmy's gang roamed mountain paths on which sheep and the year's lambs had dropped a multitude of green-black messages in an impenetrable Morse code. After tea, the back door open because of the warmth of the ever-present fire, Jac was alert for a shout from the back gate, where the gang usually gathered rather than face a furious barrage of barking by knocking Dinah's front door. On one of these occasions, he hurried the last of his milky drink, asked 'Can I go now?' and was out of the back door with his mother's 'Yes, you *may*!' trailing on the air behind him.

Eck and Billy were there, and Jimmy, who, with eyebrows restored and a surprisingly curled new forelock, was carrying a sizeable cardboard box.

'What's that for?' Jac said, after the usual brief nodded greetings. 'Are you going to collect things?'

'It's for sliding. We'll share it out, when we get to the top. You can have a bit.'

They turned their faces to the mountain and the blue sky and high white clouds. Behind them, in the valley bottom, was the defiled and mutilated landscape of pit waste, smoke and stench, the crawling terraces, the black river in the midst, and at their feet, the tufted grass and patches of emerging bracken like so many green beckoning fingers. Long accustomed to climbing the slopes, they barely noticed the stiffer steeps and were soon almost at the point where Jac remembered Jo had stood poised for a moment before plunging fleet- and sure-footed all the way to the black ash path.

Eck carried the box for a bit, then Billy. When it came to Jac, he found it so awkward and cumbersome he was in danger of tumbling backwards, until Eck noticed his predicament and shared the burden the final yards.

'Right,' said Jimmy, examining the slope to gauge its gradient and possible obstructions, 'this is a good place. All smooth and clear till you get to the quarry near the bottom.'

Jac watched with growing curiosity as, with much grunting effort, Jimmy tore the sides and separated the bottom of the box until he had two quite large portions, each with a convenient fold for holding on to, one smaller and squarish, and two decidedly small that had formed the lid. 'That'll do,' he said. 'Where's that bit of candle Billy?'

His brother rummaged in a pocket and produced a few inches of candle-end, rummaged again and from a knot of grimy handkerchief produced a smaller stump. The brothers took the larger portions of cardboard and rubbed them with wax until both were well coated, then handed the merest stubs of wax to Jac and Eck to apply to the remaining pieces.

Jimmy surveyed the effort and pronounced his degree of satisfaction. 'It's the best we can do in the circumstances. Jac you're the smallest, so you'll have to take those two small pieces. Billy, give yours to Eck, 'cause he's bigger than you.'

His brother's angry protest was swept aside and the well-waxed large portion peremptorily seized and handed to Eck, who shrugged compliance with the ruling.

'Mobile platoon … mobile platoon … mount!'

Jimmy seated himself on his cardboard, crouched forward like a starting sprinter to grasp the front edge of the sheet and, signalling the others to follow, with a couple of vigorous jerks of knees and digs of heels into the turf, set the cardboard slithering forward. Then leaning back, keeping his feet clear of the grass and the danger of spragging his forward motion, he sped down the steep slope. Eck and Billy followed Jimmy's example smoothly enough, the waxing and the dry grass reducing friction for them, too. To Jac the whole process was a revelation. But having first made do with a much diminished stub of wax, he struggled and failed to keep both smaller pieces of cardboard together and, in the end, descended slowly on one narrow strip and the seat of his trousers. Even for him, the journey to the bottom of the slope was far quicker than clambering up had been, while for the others, waiting for him and watching his unsteady progress from below, it had been exhilarating, a taste of reckless speed, before braking just in time to avoid shooting over the top of the quarry.

'That was pretty quick,' said Eck. 'Who's for another go?'

'You can see our track already.' Jimmy pointed to distinct lanes of bent grass. 'The more we slide on it, the faster it will get.' He was already on his way when he shouted, 'Who'll be first to get to the top? Come on! Keep the kettle boiling!'

The following evening, the fine, blue-bright weather holding, Jac was sitting on the warm roof of the coalhouse reading a new comic when he heard boys' voices up the mountain. He expected to see Jimmy and Billy, but he was wrong. Another gang, five strong, of about the same age, were at the top of the slide and, he guessed from their posture and actions, waxing cardboards. In a few minutes they were all whooping and yelling as they sped down the clearly marked track and braked hard to avoid the quarry. With further shouts they scrambled back up the slope, dragging their cardboards, and launched themselves into another descent.

Jac saw and heard the display of exuberant high spirits, and felt offended. 'That's our slide,' he said to himself. 'It belongs to Jimmy and Eck and Billy and me. We made it. Let 'em go back to their bit of mountain and make their own slide.' He became quite morose and went indoors to complain.

His father was getting ready for the regular evening task of ensuring Betsy had fresh feed and water for the night. 'I don't know what you expect me to do,' he said. 'Why don't you get your own cardboard and go and join them.'

'I haven't got a cardboard. Didn't have one, a proper one, before.'

'You want to go round the shops. Try asking the Co-op.'

'But they're all closed now.'

'Ah, well! You'll have to wait until tomorrow. I'll have a look round the stable. Perhaps I'll find an old box there.'

When in a while he returned, Jac was disappointed to see he had only some pieces of wood under his arm. He had found no cardboard, he said, but had an idea that might result in something better. A broken beer barrel, used long before as a water butt, though rotting where it stood, still had a few sound staves. He had prised a couple loose, and there they were, quite stout lengths of curved wood, a bit mouldy and soft at one end, but he could soon take care of that.

'I don't think I could slide on one of those,' said Jac.

His father laughed. 'No, I don't think so either. Or ski on two of them. Have you seen the photos of those soldiers in the snow, all in white, on skis? Never mind,' as Jac shook his head, 'that's not what I was thinking of anyway. Now up to the garage with us, for tools and a bit of planking.'

Dada was as deft and accurate with saw, hammer and nails as he was with petrol engines and electrical parts and connections. The skills that were innate and long practised had been enhanced by the necessity of improvisation at home and at work during the years of war shortages. Jac watched as he trimmed both staves to about two feet six inches, then measured with his eye and sawed two short lengths from a plank left over from a shelving job. Having rubbed down raw edges, he laid the staves on his workbench a foot or so apart, bridged them fore and aft with the pieces of plank, one at the very end, the other, slimmer, six inches or so in. It was only when he bored holes through the latter and the staves it was fastened to, and knotted a length of sash cord loosely across, that Jac could exclaim, 'You've made a sledge!'

'That should be better than cardboard for sliding,' his father said. 'Bit late to try now, but you could take it up the mountain tomorrow – if the weather's fine. Come on – we'll lock up here and you can take it home to show Mama.' He picked the sledge up and carried it under his arm as easily as he carried blocks of wood up from the pit.

His mother and a very tired Jo praised its construction and hailed its promise as a veritable slide express. 'Do be careful,' his mother said. 'You don't want to go over the quarry on it.'

In bed that night he thought about the impression he would make, sliding on his own sledge as the rest of the gang watched, clutching their pieces of cardboard. It was an exciting prospect and made the next school day infinitely long and tedious.

'Don't rush,' Mama said at teatime. 'Don't go making yourself ill just to go up the slide. It will be there tomorrow.'

'But it may be raining then and it's fine now. Can I go?'

His mother sighed and shook her head. *'May I ... '* she said, hopelessly, then, 'Oh, all right.'

Released, he picked up the sledge, which was leaning against the wall outside the back door, and carried it up the steps and the garden path. When he put it down to open the groaning gate he realised his arm was tired and, as he first carried, then dragged it up the diagonal mountain paths using one arm, then the other, then both while walking slowly backwards, he began to see that sliding on cardboard had its advantages.

He was sure his friends would come and at the top of the slide sat rubbing his aching arms and waiting for them. Then he thought he would have a short practice, just to feel what it was like. He moved the sledge off the narrow path to the top of the slide, which, after much enthusiastic use, was a clearly marked blond lane down the green slope. He sat on the plank seat, held the rope, just like the reins of a horse, in both hands, put his feet on the footrest and willed it to move. Nothing happened. He pulled at the rope, clicked his tongue as he had learned to do with Bonny: the sledge ignored him. He jerked his body and it slithered a yard down the slope and stopped.

Voices faintly calling down on the black ash path rose up to him. It was Jimmy and Billy and Eck at his back garden fence. He shouted to them, but they didn't hear. His mother appeared on the garden path and his friends turned together to see him at the top of the slide. They waved and shouted. He waved back. It would have been wonderful if, just then, he had been able to slide all the way down to meet them, but with more bouncing on the seat, the sledge moved forward only a couple of feet and again stopped.

They were quickly with him carrying new pieces of

cardboard. Jac had pulled the reluctant sledge back on to the path, where it attracted breathless admiration.

'What a great sledge!' said Eck. 'Where'd you get it? Bet it goes like the wind.'

'Can I have a go on it?'

'Me first, me first!'

Jac couldn't think how to answer them. The sledge looked powerful and full of speed, why then didn't it go?

'I haven't tried it yet. Perhaps you could give it a run, Jimmy ... see if it goes right.' He didn't really know what to say.

'Have you put wax on the runners? Let's have a look.'

Before Jac could answer, Jimmy turned the sledge over, with more difficulty than he anticipated. 'Blimey, it's heavy,' he said. 'Wait a minute – no, no wax.'

'My Mam said we haven't got any.' Jac was ashamed of the lie, but no one seemed to notice.

Jimmy produced a fresh stub of candle from his pocket and proceeded to rub it vigorously into the lengths of stave. 'They're off a barrel, aren't they?' he said. 'What a great idea. Look how they curve up a bit at the front. No wonder the sledge is heavy though: they're oak – and pretty thick.'

This was news to Jac, who shrugged and said nothing. Jimmy moved the sledge until it balanced on the edge of the slide, which ran down straight, palely sleek and gilded in the evening sun. He sat on the sledge holding the rope.

'Right-O. Plane cleared for take-off. Pilot at the controls. Come on, give us a little push.'

Eck bent to the task. With both hands on the back of the plank seat he pushed hard and, as the sledge moved, fell forward on to the slide.

'Ow! my nose,' he said.

Billy and Jac were more concerned with the progress of the test flight. The sledge slid forward quite slowly and then, seeming to find confidence in its own motion, gathered speed. Within twenty feet it was flying down the flaxen lane.

Jimmy's 'Halloo! Tally-ho!!' died as he neared the top of the quarry. He struggled briefly with the rope and then threw himself off the sledge just before it took to the air indeed, flew a dozen feet and crashed into the stony red gash low on the mountain's flank.

Eck sitting on the slide dabbing his nose, Jac and Billy just behind on the path, watched with a mixture of admiration and concern. The velocity of the descent had been shocking.

'Like a rocket!' said Billy, to no one in particular, and all three ran down the side of the slide to where Jimmy was sitting, nursing his wrist.

'You all right?' said Eck as they reached the fallen hero.

'Yes, I think so,' he said, and pulling himself together, '... parachute failed to open properly, but only a bent wrist. I'll manage with a sling.' He opened a button on his shirt and thrust his arm in, then took it out again to struggle to his feet. 'How's the plane? Golly, didn't it go!'

They scrambled down into the quarry, where the sledge lay upside down, displaying its bright wax- and grass-polished runners. It was clear at a glance that the footrest had broken loose on one side in the fall, but otherwise its stout structure had survived.

'I can mend it,' Jimmy said, 'when my wrist's better. Are you lot going to have a slide?'

No one was keen to carry on. There had been enough excitement.

'I think I'll go and read for a bit,' Jac said.

'Good idea. Eck, can you and Billy get the cardboards? I'll go and ask our Ma for a bandage for my wrist.' Limping slightly he made his way out of the quarry and down to the ash path.

Without a word Eck and Billy started out for the top of the slide where their new, still unwaxed cardboards lay. Jac hauled the damaged sledge by its rope over the lower lip of the quarry and down the ruggedly grassed slope below to the garden wall. His fumbling with the latch and the rackety din of the gate brought Dinah, hackles raised, to the top of the steps. Seeing nothing to stir her further to a paroxysm of fury, she sniffed the air, and slouched away disappointed, while he carried the sledge awkwardly down the cobbled path and leaned it against the low back wall of the coal shed.

'How did you get on?' his mother asked, expecting a full report. 'Was it thrilling?'

'Yes – it was quite interesting.'

'Another go tomorrow, perhaps.'

'H'm. Yes, perhaps. Have you seen my comic?'

That night it rained heavily, the prelude to days of squally showers. By the time the weather had more or less settled to something like summer again, the blanched streak down the mountain had regained its natural green and, in the annual round of activities, the time for sliding had passed.

\*

To the children at least, the war had become normal, a permanence, a fact of existence; they had known, or could remember, little else. It was the turn of German industrial centres, towns and cities to suffer mass bombing raids, and for the Russians, having survived so much devastation, to push back against the Fascist enemy. The Allies' victory in North Africa provided a springboard for the successful invasion of Sicily in July 1943 and before the end of the month Mussolini had been deposed. Italy signed an armistice agreement with the Allies, but the German forces there, now an army of occupation, fought on. Early in 1944, wireless news bulletins told how the allied advance up the shin of Italy had stalled, and in the cinema, while they waited for the *Tarzan*, or cowboy or gangster film that was the main attraction, the audience watched newsreels of bombs tumbling through smoke filled air on the great Benedictine monastery of Monte Cassino, one end of the German line. Before the conclusion of the bitterly fought campaign, the Allies would lose 300,000 killed or wounded, the German army 434,000.

*

If anyone had bothered to ask, Jac would have said he was in Jimmy's gang, Eck the same; ditto Billy, with brotherly reluctance, though even he agreed Jimmy was more familiar with the valley's nooks and crannies than anyone else he knew, and had the daring to explore beyond its confines. He also had the useful ability to shrug off mishaps, stumbles, falls, quirks of ill-fate. Setbacks of all kinds did not set him back. He simply ignored them and carried on, confident as before, in a style borrowed from heroes in comics and Hollywood films.

With war a constant, the gang continued on manoeuvres. In the third week of April, during the Easter holiday, they followed familiar paths beyond the neglected slide to the top of the mountain, where long lines of broken walls enclosed nothing but grass and rushes and bracken, and if they had paused to listen, they would have heard skylarks sing. Jimmy said it was a route march and would smarten them up, get them fit.

'We'll take turns to be on point,' he said.

'Uh?' said Eck. 'What's that?'

'In the front … leading!'

'Right. OK. Why didn't you say so? I'll start if you like.'

Jimmy's exasperation was barely concealed, but he fell in behind the volunteer point man. 'Remember, you have to set the pace … and you're the first to face incoming fire. Our objective is that big tump up the top of the valley.'

Most of the gradients on the mountain top were gentle, but Eck set off up a long, shallow slope at a pace that soon had Jimmy breathing hard and Billy and Jac trailing some distance behind.

'Platoon halt,' gasped Jimmy and, when Jac had eventually caught up, all four threw themselves down on the long, coarse grass.

'I wish I'd brought a drink,' said Billy. 'Didn't know we were going to be rushing about like this.'

'Pop,' said Jac. 'Pop would be nice now.'

'How about a cup of tea and a biscuit?' said Eck.

'No, no – it's water you should have,' Jimmy said. 'And I don't know what you're talking about anyway. We haven't got pop or tea – or water.'

'H'm, not much of a route march with no water,' said Eck. 'I'll just chew a blade of grass.'

'Right,' said Jimmy, 'on your feet. Who's taking over on point?'

'Me,' said Billy, setting off at little more than a saunter, which the others were content to follow, until Jimmy said 'Pick 'em up, pick 'em up', and he accelerated to a steady walk.

Regiments of hairy green bracken stems had sprouted among the brittle, rusted litter of last year's growth on either side of the path. Soon they would grow straight and tall (taller than Jac, some taller even than Jimmy) to palm-like clusters of broad arrowing fronds, and in the crowded patches take on a jungle density. Scruffy sheep and lambs already coal-dust grey paused in their grazing to gaze at the marching squad with unblinking, wary eyes. It was warm. The earlier breeze had run out of breath. Eck dragged his grey jumper off and, dark hair dramatically on end, used the sleeves to tie it round his waist.

At length, as they approached the closed end of the valley, the path along the undulating moorland swung nearer to the edge of the steep slope running down to the terraced houses and the pits and the railway, and the polluted stream at the bottom. The upper reaches of an enormous black slag heap with its diminutive lifting gear at the summit came into view, accompanied by the muffled clangs of tipping and puffs of dust as load after load of pit waste tumbled onto the still growing black mountain. The path bent away again and they were at the foot of the familiar lookout hill crowning the valley.

'Each man for himself up to the highest point,' said Jimmy. 'There's a sort of pillar there. You've got to touch that. Jac, we'll give you a start. I'll count to fifty and then we'll come after you.'

'What about me?' said Billy.

'Oh, OK, if you must. You can have twenty-five.'

Eck lifted his head as though measuring height and gradient, and sighed.

'Ready?' said Jimmy. 'Ready ... steady ... Go!'

Because of its steepness, Jac well knew, running down the hill would be far from easy. Running up was near impossible. Within twenty yards of digging his toes in to get some purchase on the slope, he was scrambling splay-footed and using his hands to grab tufts of grass and haul himself upwards. Soon, above the thump of pulse and his own breathing, he heard panting breath behind, and then Billy passed, swarming upwards like him. In a moment or so, while he paused, breathless, Jimmy and Eck, almost together, overtook him and he watched as their longer arms and legs pulled and thrust them towards the summit.

At the top Jac was surprised to find there was, indeed, a pillar, not visible from anywhere on the steep slope up. The rest of the gang were gathered about it, bent over, hands on knees, still gasping. He joined them.

'There you are,' Jimmy said, 'the highest point. That's the way to get fit.'

'Don't know about fit,' said Eck. 'Think I'm done for.' And he flung himself down on the grass. 'Leave me here, boys. Tell 'em back home I did my bit, and it's done me good and proper.'

'Well then – short bivouac before the next lap.' Jimmy wasn't sure about 'bivouac', but no one had the knowledge, or breath, to challenge him.

From the concrete column, only the higher reaches of the western side of the valley they had left were visible, and smoke rising from the colliery engine houses. But to the east, under blue sky and bubbling white clouds, another, larger valley had thrust its crusted fingers into the moorland. This, too, had its slowly uncoiling terraces, grey-slated roofs like sombre dragon scales on the longest of stretching limbs, and the same darkness, the same smoking trough at its core.

'Where we going?' said Jac, pointing to the almost silent township, where a sunstruck window flashed a message. 'Down there?'

'No, not straight down that way. First the pond, then,' Jimmy paused for dramatic effect, '"Ghost Town".'

Billy had some notion of this target gathered from conversations between his older brothers, but said nothing. Jac, more than half inclined to believe in ghosts, was as intrigued as he was alarmed; Eck affected nonchalance.

'Follow me!' said Jimmy, launching himself down the slope in the chosen direction, careless of consequence. The others followed, running zigzag courses to avoid tumbling in a heap to the bottom. Though careful, their descent was exhilarating, while Jimmy, waiting for them, was exulting in his speed and safe arrival at the foot of the hill. With arm aloft he signalled, 'Forward-ho!' and set off at a trot into the shallow depression that held the pond in its palm.

A large, rush-fringed oval, fully twenty yards across and thirty long, bigger than any stretch of fresh water Jac had ever seen before, it lay perfectly still, contemplating its reflection of sky and the green of the surrounding low hills. It was enticing.

'How about a paddle?' said Eck. 'I've got hot feet. I belong to the Hot-foot tribe.'

'No time.'

'Not even to dip my big toe?'

Jimmy saw the possibility of the expedition foundering. 'Ghost Town next stop,' he said, 'It's not far now. Come on. All we have to do is follow the little stream over there.'

He led them to an outlet sluice where the ponded water flowed bright and clear along a channel sloping away around a hillock, from the top of which they surveyed a cluster of buildings and, some distance off, a couple of straggling terraces and the grey glimpse of a road.

'There it is,' he said, pointing dramatically.

They continued following the stream and saw more clearly as they approached that the buildings, constructed of pink and brown brick, were whole, even to their slated roofs, except for windows broken or missing entirely, and that they had a familiar outline. There was the winding engine house, there workshops, there, towering over all, the tall, tapering chimney stack.

'It's just a colliery,' said Billy. 'We needn't have come all this way to see a colliery. We've got one at the bottom of our garden.'

'But this one is *deserted*,' said his brother, with heavy emphasis. 'Why is that, do you think?'

'The abandoned mine!' said Eck, looking closely at Jac. 'Like the good ship *Marie Celeste*. Bet it's haunted.'

'What's *Marie Celeste*?' said Jac, but no one else seemed interested.

'Perhaps there was a fire down there, underground.' Jimmy was more rational. 'That sort of thing does happen. And then because of all the coal burning, they just had to leave it and go.'

'Or a 'splosion,' Billy added. They had all heard of the terrible human cost of explosions underground.

'No. I think,' Eck said, still looking at Jac, 'they were there just digging away, by the flickerin' light of their lamps, digging with their picks, and suddenly a big piece of coal fell out and there was a scaly monster from long, long ago, and they had woken him up, and he roared, Arrh!'

Hands clawed, he mimed a pounce at Jac, who started backwards, and then laughed.

'That's rubbish,' said Jimmy. 'Don't listen to him.'

'My Grancha told me – honest now – that when he used to work underground, hacking away with his pick, he's seen live things hop out of the coal.'

'Aye, rats and black pats,' said Jimmy.

There was no one and nothing to prevent entry to any of the buildings. At first they entered blank doorways quietly and tentatively, but soon they ran from one to the other, calling out in fruitless search of an echo. All the busy machinery that had once occupied halls and smaller rooms, all the tools, everything of use or value had been hauled away.

'One thing I don't understand: how did they get to the coal?' said Eck. 'As my Grancha says "You can't dig much coal, boy bach, without a drift or a shaft to go underground".'

'I'll show you, if you like.' Jimmy smiled and led them to the doorway of the big engine house building. 'There's the shaft,' he said, pointing to a low wall some twenty yards off.

Circular and about four feet high, the wall was made of the same blend of pink and brown bricks as the buildings, but without the essential headgear for raising and lowering the cage, the others hadn't recognised it. It was too tall for Jac to see within. Jimmy and Eck could peer over the top, though without being able to see any distance down the shaft. Billy, on tip-toe, could make out a portion of wall across the circumference, but this limitation brought to his view a hole in the curve low down on the other side.

Jimmy pondered the phenomenon. Perhaps the cement

had weathered in that spot and someone had come and forced bricks apart, out of curiosity, to see if they could, and then poked at the wall until they had broken through. Anyway, there it was – a viewing place, the very thing they wanted.

The hole was just big enough to thrust head and squirm shoulders in, and Billy first, then the others in turn did that, to look down into the depths, while someone else held his ankles, just in case. What each saw clearly was some fifty feet or so of shaft, which was as far as daylight allowed, then a gradually intensifying twilight in which it was possible to make out great bars of iron or steel fallen criss-crossed and jammed within the circle, discarded remnants of the structure that once crowned it. And there was something else: in turn they heard, far, far down, the sound of water moving in the deep darkness of the pit.

That seemed to be the end of the adventure. Everyone thought of home and teatime. Except Jimmy. Without a word, he straightened himself, put both hands on top of the wall and, levering his body up, with a little scrabbling of his toecaps against the brick surface, hoisted himself so that he could place first forearms and elbows on the top and, with more effort, one knee, and then raise himself upright so that he stood on the width of two bricks outlined against the sky. On one side was the ground, where the others were watching, surprised with sudden horror, on the other, a drop of hundreds of feet into darkness and swirling water.

'What you doing?' whispered Billy. 'Come down.'

'When I'm ready,' said Jimmy, and he began a leisurely walk around the circumference of the shaft wall.

He completed half the circuit, then sat on the wall facing the engine house, its blank eyes, its brick facade more suffused with pink in the declining sun, and jumped lightly to the ground. Nothing terrible had happened, but they were all suddenly aware of the imminence of mortal danger, of death itself.

'Platoon … at ease,' he said as the others gathered silently. 'Platoon … dismiss.' And then, 'OK. Let's go home.'

Weariness had descended upon them like an ancient creature with dark, enveloping wings, and home was a long way off. Although Jimmy led them by the shortest route directly over the mountain to their own part of the valley, the journey seemed endless. Hardly a word was spoken until they separated at the neighbouring back garden gates of Eck and Jac.

'See you' they said.

'Yeh, see you.'

*

Early in June 1944, as the Allies slowly pushed north in Italy, Rome was liberated, to the immense joy of its people, but that victory was overshadowed a day later by the Allied landings on the beaches of Normandy. In all the houses in the valley, when the news came on the wireless, everyone said 'Hush' and listened intently. At nine o'clock on the evening of 6th June, the news broadcast recounted prodigious events. An armada had crossed the channel so vast it appeared a solid bridge of ships from the south coast of England all the way to France, while the sky was black with planes flying in waves to bomb Nazi coastal defences. Airborne landings had been made behind enemy lines and hundreds of minesweepers deployed to clear the way for Allied shipping. More than six hundred naval guns had bombarded the beaches before assault craft brought troops, weapons and equipment ashore. The invasion forces had suffered many casualties, and it was only the beginning but, overall, the day had gone well.

★

In the valley, on Wednesday, the day after D-Day, an unseasonably cold wind lifted puffs of black dust from the tips and tugged snorts of vapour ahead of slow-moving locomotives, but at least it was dry and a tentative optimism spread from household to household. Aunty Lil, keen to exchange the news of the moment, walked briskly through the breeze to visit her sister.

Tom had not long before lit a cheerful evening fire in the sitting room, and now, freshly bathed, hair slicked, was sharing the latest in that evening's *Echo* with Ede, as she got on with her knitting. Dinah, dozing on the hearth, was instantly roused by the clinking latch of the front gate, and would have propelled herself, bristling, to meet the intruder, but Tom stopped and held her while Edith limped to open the door at the first knock and let her sister in. As they settled to gossip together, Dinah slumped to the floor once more, head on paws, eyes closed.

Some time passed before Percy found the energy to wrap himself up and set out after Lil. He was gentle natured and it was difficult to imagine him swinging a heavy hammer, the clangour, sparks flying, or restraining a frightened horse, all part of his working day. Now, the strengthening wind seemed to snatch his breath away, though it was black dust silting his lungs that made him gasp. He chose the shorter route to the groaning back garden gate, but by the time he reached it was already tired. Slowly, warily, he walked down the cobbled path, knocked the back door gently and, finding no one answered, lifted the latch and let himself in. The kitchen was empty. He was grateful for the opportunity to sit alone for a moment in the fireside armchair and get his breath before joining the others, whose voices he could hear.

In the front room, Dinah, alerted by the faintest of sounds, struggled to her feet and ambled to the kitchen. She knew Percy, a frequent visitor, well enough but, surprised to find him in the chair by the fire, she squatted on the hearth and looked at him, her dark brown eyes unblinking.

'Hello Dinah, good girl,' said Percy, kindly, cajoling. 'They're all in the front room, are they?'

Dinah's gaze did not waver.

'Let's go in and see shall we?' He put his hands on the chair arms to raise himself.

The dog growled.

He moved his feet.

Dinah snarled, nose wrinkled, lips drawn back, white teeth gleaming.

Percy sank back in the chair.

Sometime later Tom came out to see if the kitchen fire needed attention and found the pair, Percy tense in the armchair and Dinah sitting, quietly watchful, before him.

'I didn't know you were here. We were waiting for you. Why didn't you come in,' he said.

'You'd better ask her,' Percy said, nodding in the direction of the dog.

*

Jo, who had played her small part in the manufacture of the millions of tons of munitions exploded to deadly effect in the several theatres of war, was given a day off from the factory to compensate for many hours of overtime. It was a fine pleasant day. She covered her curiously tinted hair in a turban neatly contrived from a scarf, as she did daily to go to work, and went on the bus to a nearby town where she thought to wander about and look in shop windows, simply for the pleasure of doing something normal. She had her clothes coupons with her, in case she saw something really nice she could afford, but nothing caught her eye.

Then, with no other plan in mind, she went to the market. It was not a good time for home-grown fruit, and other foods were rationed, but it wasn't food that drew her. Rather, she went to look at the few stalls where puppies and kittens could sometimes be found. She loved animals. In some senses, Betsy was her best friend, the one to whom she talked about her worries and fears and desires, talked long and confidentially, without ever being interrupted or questioned, or ever thought the worse of because of what she said.

There were puppies and kittens, but what most caught her attention was a wire cage containing three ducklings. She looked at them and smiled. It was the first time in weeks she had smiled naturally, instinctively, with the sudden surge of pleasure brought by these tiny creatures, their yellow downy feathers, bead-bright eyes, and exquisite bills. 'Oh, bless 'em. They're beautiful,' she whispered to herself. She could not leave the stall without them. They were packed into a shoebox holed at the top for air, on a bed of shredded newspaper and, for a few pence more a small bag of feed and a shallow metal bowl for water were added to her burden.

Mama shared Jo's delight in the ducklings. Her father took a more pragmatic view, but in the end it was Dinah who solved the initial problem of housing and nurturing them. She had a stout cardboard box of her own, lined with an old blanket, behind the curtained recess beside the grate in the kitchen. It had been her cwtch when she was a pup and, though too small to accommodate her adult bulk comfortably, was still the place to which she carried damply mauled newspapers and letters, if she managed to reach them first as they fell through the letterbox, which was usually the case. The recess was warm because of its nearness to the fire and, with hay brought down from the stable replacing the tattered blanket, was a suitable temporary home for the ducklings.

'What will Dinah do?' Jac asked. 'She might eat them.'

'We'll have to keep an eye on her. You never know with Dinah.'

Her mad territorial possessiveness suggested the dog might resent a newcomer, of any kind, and all three together would hardly have made a mouthful for her, but they needn't have worried. The ducklings, squeaking helplessly as they wandered about their cardboard enclosure, aroused her long-suppressed maternal instinct. Dotingly, she watched them eat the specks of food Jo put in a saucer for them and dip their beaks into the bowl of water. Then she lovingly washed them, licking with her long, wet red tongue until their fluff was plastered to their tiny bodies. The ducklings, knowing nothing to the contrary, accepted this treatment as normal, and when she settled herself in the box they lay down too, pressed against her furry belly. Within a day or so, wherever Dinah moved the ducklings followed; within a week their yellow down had disappeared and they were a uniform bedraggled grey.

Everyone knew ducks needed water for bathing and swimming. At work, Jo begged for, and at length was surreptitiously given, a metal tray, about the size of a large tea tray, but with sides of six inches or so. With a struggle, she brought it home on the crowded workers' train, dug a hole in the grass outside the back room door to accommodate it, and filled it with water. Dinah led her brood to inspect the shallow pool and lapped at it, but the ducklings knew at once what it was for, jumping in fearlessly, swimming in all directions with every indication of pleasure and startling speed, then dipping their heads in the water. In a while they emerged transformed, yellow again.

It wasn't long before the ducklings stubby first feathers appeared at breast and tail, and Dinah led them up the garden. There, as she watched, filled with pride, they fell upon vegetable seedlings and small grubs with hearty appetites. To the amusement of all who observed it, a pattern was set: the dog, calmer in her new status of foster-motherhood, kept the ducklings warm at night and seemed to enjoy being followed by them through the day. It meant she had less time and, perhaps, inclination, to shout at passers-by, and gallop, bristling, to greet any caller at the front door.

'It'll be the end of the garden,' Jac's father observed. 'They'll eat every green thing.'

'Can't you fence a part of it. It wouldn't need to be tall. Just a low fence would keep them out.'

'While they're small. Wait till their wings grow stronger. I'll ask Dic if he can build some sort of barricade and re-seed. Late salad stuff and vegetables this year.' He smiled ruefully.

'It is lovely to watch them,' Mama said.

'Yes, I suppose so.'

The coming of the ducklings brought a subtle lifting of the spirits. It was as though, that springtime and early summer, hope had been reborn. But there were hard times and horrors to come.

★

On June 13th 1944, a week after the Allied invasion of Europe, the first V1 flying bomb struck London. Soon, newsreels revealed this latest of war's ghastly novelties moving across the sky quite slowly, an almost toy-like dark echo of Flash Gordon's rocket ship, until the puttering engine stopped. Then it fell, and wherever it fell there was enormous destruction and loss of life. By the end of the month, the Nazis were launching a hundred a day towards southern England. In September, the V2 bombardment began. Unlike the V1, it could not be shot down by protective RAF fighters or anti-aircraft guns. It descended from an altitude of sixty miles at three times the speed of sound, and its one ton of explosives detonated on impact. Front pages of all the newspapers told how one fell on a crowded London Woolworth's store at half-past twelve on Saturday 25th November, and killed 173 unsuspecting shoppers.

It was one of those autumn days of constant rain, seeping from a sky that seemed to press down on the valley's chimney pots. In what remained of daylight, Jac was moping about the house and his mother was growing tired of his morose idleness.

'Why don't you go to the library and see if there's a book you like?'

Dada had signed the form for him to obtain a library card

so that he could borrow books, but he was faithful to his comics and rarely used it. He shrugged, but because he, too, was weary of doing nothing, put his mac on and his cap and walked through the steady drizzle to the Workmen's Hall. Smoke and fumes were rising from the road across the old tip like a putrid marsh mist. He was glad to get to the tall door and, at a stretch of his arm, turn the knob and let himself in. The library lights were on, it was dry, and the smell of dust and old books was strangely reassuring.

On that day he took a volume from a set on a low shelf, because it was the biggest book within reach and, to his surprise, quickly became engrossed. It was an encyclopaedia and, just as cartoon strips attracted him to stories in the comics, the illustrations drew him into the fascination of prehistory. He would have borrowed a volume, for they were full of wonders, but it was not allowed, so he read avidly, seated on an uncomfortable, straight-backed wooden chair in a corner. With such a heavy book, he was sure it would be much easier to handle, and altogether more convenient, if he sat, or lay, on the floor, but that wasn't allowed either. The librarian, a formidable, elderly lady, suspicious of the behaviour of small boys, looked at him frequently as he read, but he took no notice.

Of all the pages he turned, the most interesting were those that described the development of life on earth. Time in tens of millions of years was beyond his imagining, for he could remember only fragments of what happened one year ago, but the names alone of geological eras fascinated him as he sounded them in whispers to himself: Triassic, Jurassic, Cretaceous. They were words he had never heard pronounced in school, nor had his teachers ever mentioned dinosaurs, creatures that had lived then, long, long before man ever walked the earth. Their images in the encyclopaedia gripped him fiercely. He whispered and savoured on his tongue their awful names – stegosaurus, tyrannosaurus, and diplodocus – which he pronounced the Welsh way. He learned how their gigantic size and terrifying form were known because men and women had found and studied their fossilised remains buried in the earth all those millions of years. Later, in dreams, he saw them, scaly or plated, with their colossal bodies and tiny brains, and enormous curved teeth, and on dark evenings, after tea was cleared away leaving the kitchen table free, he modelled them using the plasticine he had received as a birthday gift.

He was already familiar with the glossy black fossil-images of fern-like vegetation imprinted on fragments of blue-grey shale on the tip of the abandoned mine just beyond the back gate where he and Eck, and Jimmy and Billy practised combat manoeuvres. Jimmy and Billy, he thought, probably knew all about dinosaurs, because Jimmy knew everything, but obsessed by war, perhaps, they simply hadn't bothered to mention them. To Jac, these creatures of the remotely distant past were suddenly far more interesting than commando training.

He was so excited by this new knowledge that when he caught Jo, tired after work, in meditative mood, he told her all about the dinosaurs.

'They were huge,' he said. 'Enormous!'

'As big as Betsy?' Jo said, slowly, indulgently. She seemed to have grown much older.

Experience of working in the factory had so exaggerated

the distance between them in years, she sometimes felt more like a second mother to him than an older sister.

'Oh, much, much bigger than Betsy. Bigger than an elephant. Bigger than ... ten elephants! And teeth on them – some of them,' he held his arms wide apart, 'long, like skimitars'.

'I think that's "scimitar",' said Jo gently. 'Oh, long and curved, like that.'

'Yes, yes,' said Jac. 'Like scimitars.'

'H'm. Well, I wouldn't want to run into one of them in the dark.'

'I'm going to search for fossils,' Jac said, '– for dinosaur fossils.'

'Where do you think you'll find them?'

'They're in rocks from under the ground – and I've seen some. Up on the old tip. They've got leaves and things, and they're on rocks brought up with the coal – from underground. I'll show you what I find.'

He shared his new knowledge with Eck also, who was immediately enthused. Soon they were practising together the monsters' names, chanting them almost like a spell: pterodactyl, tyrannosaurus, diplodocus. Eck borrowed his Grancha's hammer and they went up the old tip fossil hunting. They found that if you tapped the edge of almost any lump of shale picked up on the tip, it split easily into thin layers, which were sometimes imprinted with fern-like plants, exactly like those Jac had chanced upon before. They became absorbed in tapping and splitting, and examining what each fresh surface revealed, but very often the pages of the stony codex were fragile and difficult to extract. The best they saved with some pride.

Jac was content to go on quietly in this way, hoping among

all the fragments to come upon something more complete, more perfect, above all different, in the catalogue of fossil remains, but Eck was impatient. Like Jac, he knew nothing of geological epochs, but was excited by the notion of discovering a fossil dinosaur. Even a very small dinosaur would do.

'I bet there are better fossils on the tip by the culvert,' he said, 'fresh ones, just dug up from underground. Let's go down there.'

The story of Jac running the culvert and sliding into the stream had somehow eventually got back to his mother and father, for the valley was small and close, a place of very few secrets. It was too late then to be angry with him, but his father told him firmly that the foot of the tip, where it was penetrated by the culvert, was a dangerous place. Dram-loads of slag were constantly pitched forward from the top and heavy lumps were liable to bound and crash all the way to the bottom. If one were to hit a small boy, that would be the end of him. 'So don't you go there. Do you hear what I say?' Jac had bowed his head contritely, 'Yes, Dada.'

'I can't go there,' he said to Eck. 'I promised my father.'

'He won't know. You don't have to tell him.'

Eck's Dad, away in the war, always added to his letters home a message urging Eric to be a good boy and look after his mother, but his Grancha, while great at telling stories, especially about the old days, was not one for laying down the law about rights and wrongs.

'We won't go near the culvert. Cross my heart!' He licked a finger and made a cross in the middle of his grey jumper. 'We can look for fossils further down than that, where they've finished tipping. And we won't go by the river, honest. Fen swimming!' He laughed, and laughed again at Jac's puzzled look.

They went down the road, clicked through the station gate and over the railway lines' auburn-boarded pedestrian crossing, through another gate and down another black ash path running past the colliery. The wall on one side was pierced at intervals by circular, slatted windows, like large dirty portholes, through which drifted wisps of smoke, coal stench, occasional shouts and metallic clangs, the whirring of machinery. Looming over the wall the tall, square chimney stack, built with black bricks, encrusted with soot and black dust, trailed a grimy cloud across a sombre sky.

'It's the engine house,' said Jac. 'My father told me to keep away from here.'

'That's all right. We're not going there. Honest. Just passing by. Hello colliery!' He waved to the wall and grinned.

Despite Eck's cheerful reassurance, Jac was uneasy. At a gap in the wall, they looked across the blackened surface, with its silver scrawl of steel dram tracks leading to the dark tunnel entrance of the drift in the mountainside, still green, rising steeply above. For that moment, when he dared to look, he was glad to see there were no workers nearby, but two horses still in harness stood like statues, heads deep in nose bags, outside the stables, a long, low building on a rise a short distance away.

A narrow wooden bridge took them over the river which, swollen by recent rains, was murmuring to itself darkly. Just there, beyond the further bank, Eck led the way though a damp and rushy zone towards the foot of the embankment along the top of which filled drams were hauled up to the screens and more rapidly, and noisily, clattered empty down.

As he had said, there was no tipping going on in the place he stopped, but Jac was worried. It was far closer to the colliery than he had thought to be when they set out, the engine house even now barely a hundred yards off, and the drift entrance still visible.

Under the cloud-covered sky, the colliery and everything to do with it, still or moving, was black, coal black, including the surface workers themselves, busy at their jobs. Jac wondered whether his father, whose skills were needed in all parts of the colliery, would be among them. He was troubled by what might happen if Dada saw him.

'I don't think we're allowed b'ere,' he said. 'What if drams come down?'

'They don't run here,' said Eck. 'They don't crawl along the side of this bank like flies. They're on the top, aren't they? Up there.' He pointed to the crown of the great extended pile of pit waste, where they saw a pair of wires strung on posts running its length suddenly begin vibrating, while somewhere a little way off among the colliery buildings a bell rang twice.

'Let's just have a quick look. P'raps there's marvellous fossils just waiting ...'

He stopped and frowned. A distant drumming further up the incline was getting louder, with an accompanying metallic clatter. What he said next was swallowed by prolonged hollow booming and rattling as empty drams, ten or more linked together, there was no time to count, sped past. Jac leapt back and crouched among the rushes.

If Eck, too, was shaken by this noisy apparition he didn't show it. Jac looked up to see him standing to attention, saluting as it rumbled past. The chain of drams, slowing, dipped out of sight, then reappeared to halt near the entrance to the drift.

'Duw, that was a nice surprise for us.' He imitated his grandfather's accent and calm way of greeting anything out of the ordinary. 'Now it's over, no harm done, we can get on.'

Jac was far less sanguine, but allowed himself to be drawn back to the foot of the embankment. It was made of black rubble, hard compacted ash from the engine house and pit waste. At first glance it seemed promising, but they soon found there were no lumps of shale like those on the familiar old tip that could be easily split to reveal imprints of the past, long, long before man ever walked the earth. Or, if any such were to be found, it would only be by delving deep within the firmly packed mass. They had no tools for digging; it was a hopeless quest. The day had darkened perceptibly; lights on posts all around the colliery surface suddenly came on together.

They trudged home disappointed, but with imaginations still full of dinosaurs and fossil-hunting.

'We can try other old tips,' said Eck. 'There's much bigger ones up the top of the valley.'

'I'll ask my father,' said Jac. 'Perhaps he knows of a good place to find fossils – where it's safe.'

Eck looked dubious. 'Yes, perhaps. If he'll tell you.'

It was a lesson renewed over and over, of ambition thwarted, reality falling short of an imagined outcome, promising plans come to naught. But you carried on: 'Grin and bear it' had joined the list of watchwords for the times. The days became shorter, the weekends dismal with rain and cold winds. Fossil hunting was not forgotten, but indefinitely postponed.

★

The war was a constant, with the sense of a gathering wave that must sometime break, but beset by cross-currents and delaying obstacles. In December, during another bitter winter, the news on the wireless and in cinema newsreels told how German forces in the Ardennes, a rugged, forested area not far from the border of their homeland, counter-attacked and drove the Allies back in what became known as the Battle of the Bulge, with terrible losses on both sides. On Christmas Eve, doodlebugs, launched now not from ground emplacements but from enemy planes over the east coast of England, struck as far north as Manchester. In the valley, as elsewhere, it was the most austere of Christmases, but people were grateful to be alive, by their warm fires, in homes still untouched by war. The new year, 1945, began with a cold, strengthening wind from the north, which persisted day after day, and then, following a lull when the weather seemed unable to make up its mind, returned straight from the Arctic with snow on its breath. So much fell that, as the end of January approached, the valley was blockaded by snow. Going out anywhere – to work, to school, to the shops for rations, to feed the restless horse in the stable, was a hardship. But it was as nothing compared to the suffering of millions across Europe as the war entered its final phases. The Allies crossed the Rhine at Remagen and established a bridge to transport men and materials. February newsreels showed squadron after squadron of bombers taking off to raid the German city of Dresden, and the myriad flashes of exploding bombs and dreadful fires lighting up the night black screen. Air crews returned to base reported the blaze was visible from a hundred miles away. In April, between the supporting feature and the main film, if they dared lift their eyes to the screen, audiences saw footage of British forces in northern Germany entering Belsen, a concentration camp where heaped thousands of skeletal prisoners lay dead and thousands more were dying. On 21st April the Russian army reached Berlin.

★

In the valley, April weather was unusually settled. After the sullen cold of a long winter, days of summer-like heat and warm showers released an explosion of green things. One Saturday afternoon, after a confining damp morning, as smoke from the pits spiralled white into blue skies, and the mountain displayed its inviting fresh sheen, the spirit of adventure returned to Eck. Safely on his side of the garden wall, his head alone in view, he shouted, 'Jac! Jac!', until Jac's mother heard, and a short while afterwards, the two boys met outside their respective back gates.

'Are we going to call for Jimmy and Billy?' were Jac's first words.

Although he had known the brothers who lived across the road long before Eck tumbled into his life, it was with him Jac felt more at ease. Their friendship had been spiced with moments of excitement and concern, but was somehow relaxed, natural, more fun.

'Let's just look for fossils,' Eck said. 'Up the tip. If we find a good one, we could tell Jimmy. Bet he'd be interested then. Anyway, it wouldn't matter. I'd like to find some for us. I told my Grancha about dinosaurs. He said he'd never seen anything like that when he was working underground. But then he said, "You never know, there's all kinds of things down there – in the dark" and he winked.'

Jac pondered this. Did Eck's grandfather mean there *might* be fossils of strange creatures down there where miners hacked away at the black seams? His father had never mentioned anything of that sort. But perhaps it was because Dada wanted him to stay away from the colliery.

'I got a great idea,' said Eck. 'You know that level up the mountain. Bet there's fossils lying round in there, just waiting for us.'

'But it's all bricked up. You can't get in. And you said it had skeletons.'

'No, I didn't. My Grancha said it. And I don't believe him. He's just teasing, my Mam says.'

'You can't get in there, anyway.'

'I think we could try,' said Eck. 'Look: you remember that shaft in Ghost Town, with the wall around it – that Jimmy walked on.'

Jac shivered. 'Yes, I remember.' He hadn't had nightmares about it, but had often thought, in the calm middle of a day, while contentedly doing something totally normal, what a terrible thing it was for Jimmy to do that.

'You know how we took turns looking down the shaft, and I held your feet so you could look? Because the wall was broken – the bricks had moved, fallen in or something, and there was a hole at the bottom.'

Yes, Jac remembered that – and peering into twilight, then darkness, deeper in the earth than he had ever imagined it was possible to go, and the criss-crossed steel beams and the faint trickling sounds of water moving. There was a good deal about that expedition that he would have preferred to forget.

'Well,' Eck went on, 'some of the bricks on the entrance to

the level are loose. I've been up there and looked. I think we could get in, if we – sort of – helped them.'

Jac looked doubtful, but said nothing.

'Come on. Let's give it a try, is it? Just a look, anyway.'

'I'd better tell my mother where we're going,' said Jac.

'Tell her you're looking for fossils,' said Eck. 'She'll like that.'

Jac retraced his steps to the back door, stretched to open the latch and called in, 'Mama'. But his mother wasn't in the kitchen. Jo was there, not long up, having enjoyed the luxury of a long sleep after night shift, through all Saturday morning and a good part of the afternoon.

'Tell Mama I'm going up the mountain a little bit.' He pointed vaguely, 'With Eck. Not far. We're going to look for fossils.'

'Oh, yes,' said Jo, still only half awake. 'Well, good luck. Watch out for those dinosaurs.'

She was sitting in Mama's usual place, in the easy chair by the side of the fire, which had been banked up with small coal. She looked at him and smiled. 'I'll tell Mama,' she said. 'Ta-ta for now!' and she smiled again.

Eck was waiting for him on the black ash path, burdened with tools, having learned the lesson from their previous fossil-hunting expedition.

'I borrowed them from my Grancha,' he said. 'He won't mind. Can you carry these? I think he said this one is a lump hammer and this one's a bolster. I thought those were for sleeping on in bed.'

He handed Jac the hammer and a broad-bladed blunt chisel.

'I asked him what you used for knocking down brick

walls – and he showed me. An' I've got a crowbar – look, just like a jemmy that burglars have in the comics – and a sack for putting fossils in.'

'That's a funny looking sack,' said Jac, weighing the hammer in his hand and finding it very heavy, 'it's got patterns.'

'It's a cushion cover really. But my Mam isn't using it. It was in her sewing basket. An' I've got this.' He reached into the bag and produced a black, box-like torch with the lens at the front, and handle at the top, and a screw to turn it on and off. 'My Dad uses it on his bicycle – when he's home,' Eck said, with a momentary wistful look. 'Cm'on, let's see if any of those bricks have fallen out.'

Galvanised beyond inhibition by Eck's enthusiasm, Jac took a firm grasp on hammer and chisel and Eck his bag and crowbar and they walked the path to the top of the familiar grey shale tip, clambered up the bare red stony bank that was the diminishing tail of the quarry, and on to the coarse grass of the mountain. A scramble of no more than twenty feet of steep slope, hampered by the weight and clumsiness of the tools, brought them to the edge of a dip towards the brick face of the abandoned level. From this vantage point, they could see there had once been a path, the route of a narrow tramway that wound diagonally down towards the low walls and the great iron wheel that were all that remained of the failed colliery's engine house.

The mountain rose above, dotted with grazing dirt-grey sheep and slightly less grubby lambs, to blue sky and a great bubbling mass of slow-moving cloud. The valley behind was Saturday quiet, which is to say, still visited by sporadic clangs and hoots and clatters, but not the constant, noisy busyness of weekdays. Within the dip, out of the slight breeze, they faced the low, tunnel-shaped brick wall that covered a former entrance to the mine. The wall appeared sound.

'I can't see that any of the bricks have moved,' said Jac.

'Well, not moved exactly. But look – down in this corner,' said Eck, twti-ing down. 'See, the cement is breaking and falling out.'

He brandished the crowbar and poked vigorously between the bricks. Very soon cement did, indeed, fall out. 'There you are: what did I tell you?' he said, and went on digging at the crevice he had created.

Jac was doubtful about the entire operation, but watched transfixed as the first loosened brick was levered out of the wall.

'Why don't you have a try with the hammer and chisel?' said Eck. 'Bet that would work a treat.'

Though still uncertain, Jac knelt by the wall, chisel in his left hand, heavy hammer in the right. Adjusting his grip on the handle of the hammer near the blunt head, the only way he could manage it at all, he tried to strike the chisel, which he had positioned between two bricks above the gap Eck had made. He struck the target at an angle, knocked the chisel sideways and immediately dropped the hammer to thrust his tingling right hand into his armpit.

'That didn't work too well,' said Eck. 'Here, let me have a go.'

He took the tools, placed the chisel on the very slight visible mark Jac's attempt had made and struck it a smart blow. To his surprise, and Jac's astonishment, one brick sprang out, dislodging its neighbour in the process.

'That's more like it!' said Eck. 'Now we're in business.'

Jac was about to ask what business, but Eck had energetically set about prising at the loosened brick with his crowbar, until quite quickly it, too, fell out of the wall. This seemed to inspire him and in a small frenzy of activity, now hammering the chisel head, now digging in and opening gaps with the crowbar, he created a hole through which he peered into the tunnel. A gasp of tainted air like a decaying sigh issued from the hole.

'Where's that torch?' he asked himself, fumbling in the cushion-cover bag to retrieve it. 'Right then, let's have a look.'

Jac was worried. 'What can you see? Is there a flood?'

'Can't see much at all. But no water. Not here anyway – so far as the light shows. We're going to have to make the hole bigger.'

'P'raps I should ask my father,' said Jac.

Even without water washing against the wall on the other side, he felt out of his depth. But Eck had nothing more to say. He picked up the tools and set to work. As is often the case, the initial breach having been made, the bond that held the wall whole broken, it became easier to loosen further bricks. Eck swung the heavy hammer at them, prodded and levered them with the crowbar, hacked with the chisel at the firmer joints, until he had created a hole down to ground level large enough to crawl through.

'Who's in first?' he asked, and immediately answered himself, 'I am!'

Then, 'Don't go,' he said to Jac, who, he saw, was on the point of leaving. 'I need you to hand me the sack and the torch, and the hammer.'

With that, he disappeared into the black, brick-fringed hole, leaving Jac to peer in after him and, in a moment or two, pass the sack with its heavy contents to the hand that emerged from the darkness.

'Ow!' said Eck, his voice echoing inside the tunnel. 'Oh, blimey, I knocked my knee. There's a rail track in here. That's better. I can stand up. Come on in. It's all right. Honest.'

Still wary about floating skeletons, Jac crawled into darkness feebly lit by Eck's torch. 'I don't think I like this,' he said.

There was air, but it was laden with damp staleness and, as they stood together, Jac instinctively reached out to hold his friend's arm.

'You all right?' said Eck.

'Mmm.' The reply was not confident.

'Look where we are.'

Eck directed the torch light in a slow arc. It revealed, below, dim reflections from a damp black surface and, close to the right of where they stood, a pair of rail tracks running away down a slight gradient and soon disappearing into black nothing. To the sides and above, the tunnel was brick lined for a yard or so only and, where the brickwork ended, the sides and roof were of hacked rock supported at intervals by stout wooden pillars flush against the squared-off walls, topped by crudely-jointed roof pieces. Still close, very close to the surface, with faint light intruding from the hole Eck had made, they stood in the silence of the pit, which was not utterly silent, but broken by noises that might have seemed unearthly, though they were truly of the earth – water dripping, here in large single drops, there in a quick patter, and the creaking of timbers bearing the weight of the mountain on their square shoulders. Between the rails at their feet, the weak illumination picked out a length of rusted wire rope that vanished suddenly like a conjuring trick.

When Eck stepped within the parallel lines of track and walked a few yards forward, taking the narrow beam of light with him, Jac followed, hurrying to keep up.

'I think we've gone far enough,' he said. 'I can't see any fossils. And it's teatime. Let's go home, is it?'

Eck was beginning to enjoy himself. 'A little bit further,' he said. 'Let's find out where this rope goes to.'

They could both see the rope was not lying along the ground, but taut and rising gradually. It was attached to something deeper in the intense black beyond the pale beam of light. Yard by yard, the tunnel through the rock was heading down into the mine. In another twenty yards or so, the track where they were treading began to bend slowly like an iron bar, and the angle of the taut rope became somewhat steeper.

'Whatever it's fixed to can't be far off,' said Eck. 'Let's find out what it is, then we'll go back. Promise.'

If the light had been stronger, they would have known before they almost walked into it. A large black object, barely distinguishable in the enveloping dense darkness, lay diagonally across the track. It was a dram, partly off the rails.

'I wish we had a bit more light,' said Eck as the torch picked out the wheels of the dram, figures and letters in chalk scrawled on the sides, and the link where the rope was attached, and then played dimly over the surface of the contents. The dram was almost full, though whether of coal or shale waste it was impossible to tell for the damp dust that covered all.

He scrabbled in it a little, then exploded. 'This is no good. There may be great fossils in this dram, but I can't see because the torch is no good. Come on!' he said and gave it an admonitory shake. The light went out.

The utter darkness that followed, in which not even the

hand touching your face was visible, was accompanied by complete silence. The dripping had strangely stopped, and the creaking of timbers. It was like the end of the world, or the blank universe before the first star was made.

The only sound that eventually broke the silence at the edge of nothing was quiet sobbing.

'Don't cry, Jac.'

'But how will we find our way out? And what about the skeletons?'

'I know a way. The skelintons won't have us. Don't cry. Just hold your hands out and move them around and I'll do the same.'

The first contact was a renewal of life. In the uttermost impenetrable black, they grasped and held on to one another, and Jac's weeping grew louder, as the terror of being blind and alone subsided.

'One last minute,' said Eck, 'and then we'll start. Hold tight to my jumper.'

He felt along the dram and then down to its wheels and the track below, drawing Jac with him.

'Can you feel those rails?'

There was a moment when the sobbing increased, then a surprised small voice, 'Yes, yes, I can feel one.'

'Try to get between them. All right? Now I'm going to empty the tools out of the sack. I don't know what Grancha will say, but it can't be helped. Wait a minute. Right. Now can you feel the sack?'

'Ye-ye-yes. There's something still in it.'

'That's nothing. Don't worry about it. Just hold on and we'll crawl. We can't get lost because we're both holding the sack and we're following the rails. You can close your eyes if you like, because it doesn't make any difference, as long as we both hold the sack and keep moving up the slope, and never go outside the rails.'

The invisible ground was wet and soft, except where scattered, fallen lumps of coal or shale grated against and grazed bare knees. Concentrating with all his might, Jac no longer sobbed, but every movement was fraught with terror of the unseen, unknown. He grasped a corner of the sack fiercely as he shuffled forward.

After a few minutes of painfully slow and awkward progress, Eck said, 'This isn't going to work. We can't crawl properly while we're holding on to the sack. I wish we had a bit of rope. But we haven't. So I'm going to whistle or sing or something as I crawl. I won't crawl fast and you keep as close as you can behind me. Can you let go of your end now?'

Releasing his hold on the cloth corner with its comforting texture of raised stitching seemed to Jac like letting go on life, and images of floating skeletons rose again on the black before his eyes. He began to sob once more.

'Come on, Jac, it's not far. Really, really not far. Listen I'm whistling.'

The whistle was a tuneless, almost soundless, blowing through Eck's pursed lips, but Jac heard it and it was somehow cheering.

Although on hands and knees, scanning the darkness with invisible fingers to touch invisible rails, made the way seem endless, it wasn't far to the entrance of the level and when, still close one behind the other, they rounded the slight bend in the track suddenly there was a gleam in the dark. The sun was beginning to decline over the mountain to the west and a shaft of light travelling to the opposite, eastern side of the valley had found the ragged opening in the bricked entrance of the level.

'There it is,' said Eck. 'Can you see it Jac?'

'Yes. Oh, yes, I can see it!'

'Keep crawling,' said Eck, 'just a bit more, until we can see the track. So we don't run into the timbers on the side.'

In a little while they glimpsed the sullen glint of rusted rail and rose to their feet and stumbled as though yet learning to walk towards the entrance and bent again and crawled through into light and evening air.

As they reached the lip of the shallow drop to the level entrance, they saw, a few yards below them on the mountain, Jac's father and Jo.

'There you are. God, what a state you're in.'

It was only then that the two boys looked down at their filthy clothes and shoes, their black hands, their black and bloody knees.

'We've been waiting for you. Looking for you. Thank goodness Jo thought you might have come up here. Your mothers have been worried sick.'

Downcast, heads lowered, neither Eck nor Jac had anything to say. They limped down to the ash path and past the fossil tip to the neighbouring back gates in the same silence, raised a hand by way of farewell to one another and parted, Eck with the cushion-cover sack over his shoulder.

Jac searched for and found his father's hand. At the creaking gate, Dinah appeared, sniffed at his muddied form suspiciously and turned away. Jac began to sob again thinking what Mama would say when she saw him and the state he was in. Jo tapped him gently on the shoulder and whispered, 'It's all right, as long as you're safe.'

She was right. He didn't have the expected row. Everyone could see he'd had a real fright, and Mama was inclined to blame Eck, who was older and should have had more sense. 'But we were only looking for fossils,' Jac pleaded.

'Perhaps that will teach you,' Dada said. 'Whatever you do, don't go down the pit.'

*

In the third week of April 1945, the Russians entered a devastated Berlin, where fighting continued from street to street. On the last day of the month Hitler committed suicide. On Monday, 7th May, Germany surrendered. Jac, on his way home from school dinnertime the next day, saw groups of women talking on the pavement and over front garden fences. 'The war's definitely over,' he heard one say. 'I've just listened to Churchill on the wireless. It's really over – at last. We can celebrate tonight.' Her neighbour said, 'A nice cup of tea will do for me.' They both laughed and everyone he saw was smiling. War against the Empire of Japan, having brought its share of grief to families in the valley, continued until the destruction of Hiroshima and Nagasaki by atomic bombs on the 6th and 9th of August, which led to the unconditional surrender of Japanese forces on the 14th of the month. A Home Guard parade was swiftly organised. Smart in khaki, the men marched all around the valley in remarkably good order, preceded by cadets beating drums and blowing trumpets, from time to time with some semblance of a tune, past flags hanging from windows and bunting suspended from lamp posts. Street tea parties were held for the children, with iced buns and pop. While beer and money lasted, men reeled happily home from pubs.

Jac's father thought it would be nice to have a big dinner to which Lil and Percy, and near neighbours, might be invited, and proposed the ducks as the centrepiece. He knew a lot of people who would appreciate a slice or two of plump duck and, suffused with the glow of victory, outlined his plan to the family. They must have seen the garden was suffering. Old Dic with his rattling chest and dreadful cough had decided, very reluctantly, for the few bob he earned meant a great deal to him, that he could no longer help to maintain the vegetable plots, but there was no point in getting someone to take his place when the fully-grown ducks were nibbling away at every green shoot. It had been lovely watching them and all that, but they would have to go some time, so … you know … wasn't this just the right celebratory occasion?

His argument had been prepared carefully, but Jo and Mama were aghast at the thought and the ducks survived. To settle the point, for a shilling, Jo bought an unwanted zinc bath from a family up the road, dug a hole to accommodate it where Dic's straddling bean sticks once stood in a line at ease, and filled it with water. The ducks were highly appreciative. One of them had acquired the habit of perching on the edge of the wall overlooking the yard and the back door, flapping its wings and quacking loudly. Dinah usually responded to the call by struggling her bulk up the steps and leading the trio in single file on a long inspection of the garden's nooks and crannies, where slugs and snails were to be found, a delightful addition to their menu. Foster-motherhood had bestowed a calming effect on Dinah's worst excesses, but she was still capable of alarming, if not terrifying, visitors.

In ones and twos, men who had been in the Forces returned to the valley. Some did not come home. For the families of the airman shot down over Hamburg, the soldier blown up by a mine on the advance through Italy, the sailor who went down with his torpedoed ship in the Far East, and others, whose grief was still raw, it was as though the longed-for peace had killed their loved ones again. But Freddy came back and there was celebration in the grey rough-cast house over the road, and older, leaner versions of the men who had long before opened the Italian corner shops were suddenly behind their counters once more.

Quite unexpectedly, Corporal Roberts turned up next door, fell into the warm embrace of his aged father and was received with relief and joy by his wife and son, whom he soon gathered up to return with him to Swindon and normal working life. On the morning before they left, Eck called over the wall for Jac and they met as before out on the path at the back of the houses.

'I've got this for you,' said Eck, handing over a lump of grey shale. 'I picked it up off the dram – before the torch went out. Remember?'

Jac remembered, all too well, the looming shape of the dram, the sudden utter blackness. 'Don't know what it is. Nothing much, I 'spect. Probably nothing at all. My Dad doesn't know, nor Grancha. But it's got marks. If you wet it a bit …'

He let a dribble of spit fall on the stone and rubbed it over the surface. '… See?'

There were, indeed, marks, faintly raised, radiating curved lines, like veins, darker than the grey matrix. 'It's not a dinosaur, that's a sure thing,' said Eck, and laughed. 'But it's a sort of souvenir of our ...' He couldn't think what to call their journey together into and out of darkness.

'Oh, it's great,' said Jac. 'Thanks. Are you going to come back?'

'Don't know ... P'raps. To see how Grancha's getting on. I better go.'

They stood looking at one another for a moment, but neither knew what to say or do next. They hadn't yet learned the parting ceremony of shaking hands, and friendly, back-slapping embraces were unknown, unheard of. With a sort of half-hearted wave, a flap of a hand, Eck turned and in a moment was gone.

The strange fossil was placed outside on the kitchen windowsill, where, slicked by rain, its faint arcing lines held the fragmentary suggestion of a winged form. Within one bolder curve lay a network of cells of infinite delicacy, as though sketched by an angel in a reverie, but no-one knew what was meant by those tantalising curves, what it might once have been. Perhaps nothing, or some freak of vegetation from the Carboniferous. Like the bomb fragment, it disappeared eventually, as though wearied of lack of recognition it had gone back into earth, or simply flown away.

A considerable time passed before Jac ventured up the mountain again to see the old level. When he did, he was surprised to find the entrance completely buried under red stony soil carried up from the quarry. It was sealed for good and, with skulls and bones still sometimes bobbing up the wormholes of his imagination, he was relieved.

★

Once the war with Germany had ended, Jimmy's military manoeuvres, having lost all purpose, to no one's regret lapsed entirely. He was seen leaving Saturday matinée with a fair-haired girl from the top of the valley. Billy was suddenly almost as tall as his brother, and more independent and cheerful, with friends who shared his cartoon-fed interest in drawing.

Jac, too, found new friends, one of whom had a football, originally the possession of an older brother, who, after war service, had moved on and away. The panelled ball, which had languished for years at the back of a cupboard, deflated and somewhat mildewed, but *real leather*, was revived by the application of dubbin. More remarkably, its pink bladder had survived unperished. Pumped up and laced tight, the ball looked a little misshapen but almost like those pictured in the boys' comic stories. The new gang played together with a great deal of enthusiasm on a stony, sparsely-grassed, uneven patch of ground behind a chapel. It was far from ideal, but the only more or less flat surface available. Discarded jumpers served as goalposts, leading to heated debates about whether a goal had been scored. The game was crude but exciting: everybody ran after the ball, hacking at it if it came within reach, and they became used to spending a lot of time and breath running down a bank to retrieve it. Jac wanted football boots for his birthday. In those times of austerity just after the war there were none to be had, but a pair of good enough boots were waiting for him on the day, with football studs nailed to soles and heels on Dada's last. The main thing, his mother thought with satisfaction, was that he was playing with boys of his own age.

As soon as she was able, Jo left the ordnance factory. She enjoyed 'potching about the house', she said, while she looked for a job with normal hours, one that would allow her summer evenings and weekends for riding over the mountains. In a little while her skin and hair recovered their normal colour. Jo had that cheerful energy that Mama had admired in her mother-in-law, who would sing joyful hymns as she cooked and cleaned. Polished surfaces were constantly hazed with dust from open fires and the first job every day was to take a soft rag and rub everything to a shine again. When Jo was cleaning, brass dresser-drawer handles rattled so with the vigour of her attack it made one smile.

Jac's mother and father wanted nothing more than to be allowed to do their share of what was needed to keep the family close and, with the Good Lord's help, not overburdened by cares. With housework shared, Mama was given a little more time for herself. She played the piano, or, so long as it wasn't raining, she enjoyed sitting in the doorway of the back room, usually with a piece of embroidery she was working on in her lap. She might glance down at Dinah dozing and twitchily dreaming, as dogs do, by her side, and then look out to a plot in the garden where a duck-proof fence had been erected to allow flower seedlings to sprout and flourish, and beyond that to the garden wall against which a frail lilac tree had somehow contrived to survive and, in spring, shyly unveiled its cones of white blossom. And, from time to time, she would raise her eyes from her needlework to the mountain, scarred to be sure, but still a living, breathing green, and listen to a blackbird, which despite the dust and noise of the colliery, only across the road on the other side of the house, still sang, oh, so beautifully.

Also by the author:

£9.99

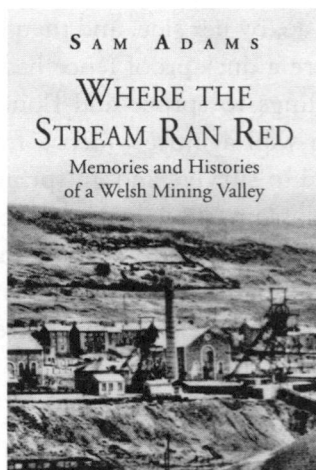

£9.99

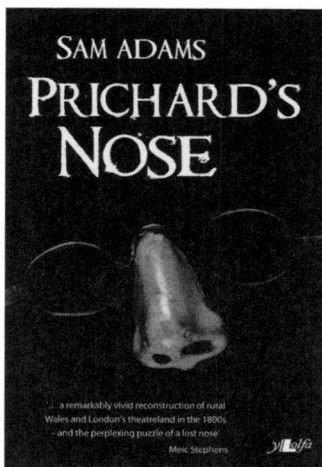

SAM ADAMS

PRICHARD'S NOSE

'a remarkably vivid reconstruction of rural
Wales and London's theatreland in the 1800s
– and the perplexing puzzle of a lost nose'
Meic Stephens

y Lolfa

£9.95

SAM ADAMS

Missed Chances

y Lolfa

£5.95